CLOSE QUARTERS

SOE CIRCUIT FORTUNAE BOOK 3

THOMAS WOOD

BOLEYNBENNETT PUBLISHING

This book is a work of fiction. Names, characters, places, and incidents either are products of the author's imagination or are used fictitiously. Any resemblance to actual persons, living or dead, events, or locales is entirely coincidental.

Thomas Wood

Cover Design by Olly at MoreVisual Ltd.

Visit my website at www.ThomasWoodBooks.com

Printed in the United Kingdom

First Printing: September 2020
by
BoleynBennett Publishing

The Circuit Fortunae Series

Into the Storm (Prequel)

Don't Look Back

Playing with Fire

Close Quarters

Other series by Thomas Wood

Gliders over Normandy

The Trench Raiders

Alfie Lewis Thrillers

1

The November twilight seemed particularly cruel on my extremities as I started to fumble around in the near-total darkness. We had been laying up outside for the best part of an hour, in which time the inactivity of the tips of my fingers had caused them to turn to a blue, rivalled only in its purity by a bright, clear summer's sky.

My nose too had reddened significantly and, as yet another torrent of mucus tumbled from my nostrils, I had to make a concerted effort not to sniff it back upwards, for fear of making too much noise. Everyone else was having the same issues and managing to remain respectfully quiet as we went about our various tasks. All the while, however, I felt my state of mind becoming more and more frustrated.

Along with the chilling air, that was biting at my

mind, was the annoyance of the labels. It appeared to me that they were so stubborn to let go of the crates that they clung to, that they would never give themselves up. They clung to that last string of adhesive that they could find, until they became detached silently, a muffled breath of victory escaping my lips.

They were stubborn, made even more difficult by the fact that my fingers felt as if they could drop off at any second. For some reason, it felt to me like the Germans almost didn't want the labels to come off the soggy crates, all stacked high in the room.

I took a breath as I stepped back, desperately clutching hold of the label now in my hands, expelling the air in a cloud of condensation that disappeared as quickly as the rush of warmth that circulated around my stomach momentarily.

There was a fragile silence in the building, as if the air itself was holding its breath, waiting for the slightest noise that could plunge everything into chaos. It was that chaos, the one that I had come to both love and fear, that I prayed would never descend tonight. I was too tired, too exhausted to really fight my way through.

The only noise apparent in the room was the slight scratching, like a colony of rats all nibbling away at a farmer's stores. Just like an aggrieved farmer, I was hoping that the Germans would be just as incensed at the hordes of vermin that had snuck into that building.

It made me feel fortunate, to hear the others going

about their work, as it meant that I wasn't alone. It was a real fear that I had realised in the last couple of weeks, as if at any moment the game would be up, and all my friends would abandon me to my own devices. It was a dream that had haunted me many times, but my subconscious had ramped up its efforts in the last ten days or so.

I held the label outstretched as I stared at it in marvelment. It was a real skill to get one of these off without tearing or scrunching it up, but it was the most vital part of the entire operation. Because, once the label had the slightest tear, or minutest crumple in its corner, it looked as though it had been tampered with.

I read it with intrigue as I wondered about the man that had written on it. The top left of the label had a box for the name of the item, next to which was another with the quantity in the shipment. Below was the name of the civilian who had overseen its packing up, next to the signature of a German who presumably had inspected the contents. Underneath that was the most important of all; its destination.

This particular shipment of two hundred and fifty carburettors, signed by Raymond Peintre and Leutnant Herbert Schiff, was headed back to the Fatherland, specifically *Dusseldorf*.

I slapped it down on to another crate on the other side of the room, before peeling off yet another one that was bound for *Essen* and switching them over.

I felt quite happy with my handiwork and took a

moment to step back and admire it. It was perfect. There didn't seem to be any marks or signs that the labels had been switched over, at least not in the dingy light of the railway shed that we were scurrying about in.

I smiled slightly as I congratulated myself on a job well done, hoping that the task of remedying our deception would take a minimum of a couple of weeks. In which time I was hoping desperately that the war would be coming to an end.

Another cloud of breath was expelled from my lungs, but this time I watched it as it dissipated into the cold air, slowly funnelling upwards towards the rusting corrugated iron roof that was rather haphazardly pulled on.

Fortunately, the drizzle that had plagued our stint outside waiting for the time to strike had eased off significantly, so it was an opportunity for us all to try and dry off, even though the old, cracked bricks seemed defiant to cling to the chill of the night more than a new mother to her child.

The building must have been around for decades, as it was beginning to fall apart at every angle from which one would look. But it played to our advantage, as it meant that it was built long before the German occupation of France. That meant that it had been far easier to gain entry to it than the Germans would perhaps have liked.

Having said that, it had seemed curious to me that

so few guards had been placed in its vicinity, most of the sentries instead opting to keep watch from the station platform, where hot coffee and other luxuries could presumably be found.

The ease with which we had slipped in unnoticed was welcome in more than one regard. It meant that we had a lot longer to organise ourselves once inside, but also it was a useful way for both Mike and me to warm up to our new area. It was an easy operation to begin with, in which we knew we were carrying out a harassment of the Germans that they were not even aware of, but also taking it as an opportunity to observe our new comrades, and to work out how they ticked.

Most of them had seemed like decent, switched on men so far, their motivation for causing havoc driven by their hatred of the occupying Germans, and that was good enough for us.

They too were walking around with large grins on their faces, as they switched Fritz's replacement car parts with a crate of trousers addressed to Hans. The only regret was that I would not be anywhere near the intended recipients as they realised what had happened, so that I would be able to see their faces.

Instead, I would be sat a couple of hundred miles away, in *Besançon*, a quaint French village that I had been forced to call my new home. We had been forced to move away, to find somewhere else to harass the Germans, on account of the fact that things had become rather hairy back in *Tours*, where we had spent the last few months of our lives.

We had both felt rather exposed after the showdown with the two *Gestapo* officers, only just escaping with our lives.

Our work there would have been suffocated if we had stayed, and the circuit that we had helped to build up was in tatters, with a series of locals who had been at the top slowly being incapacitated in one way or another. The circuit then, had been closed down as a result, but I had no doubts in my mind that the local French men would carry on in their struggle against the Germans. But this time they would have no assistance from the Brits.

I presumed however that they would get on just fine without us. I had long suspected that we had been treading on their toes anyway.

Now, we had a new priority, with new targets and new aims. The revised and relocated *Fortunae* circuit was now in full flow, with their two agents that would act as their mentors and link to London, until such a time that we would end up in trouble again.

It was a fear that would hang over me for a long time, feeling as though I was some kind of a liability to these people, an omen. I had overseen the deaths of many French people, both good and bad, but all of them in most regrettable circumstances. It was in their memory that I had determined to draw my motivation, particularly for Suzanne, and for Alfred.

A dark face peered around a corner towards me,

so shadowy and featureless that he almost appeared as a figment of my nightmares. But there was no mistaking the mischievous grin that flashed across his face momentarily. I had seen it whilst sitting outside a dispersal hut just outside of London, I had even seen it when in the thick of the action in central France, but it filled me with great joy to see it once again in the railway shed near *Besançon.*

"How are you getting on, old fruit?" he breathed, his rancid breath thankfully dissipating into the darkness as mine had done seconds ago.

"Good," I breathed back, expelling just as much awful breath into his face. "How are you doing?"

"It feels mightily good to be back, doesn't it?" I smiled at him, his grin infectious and warm, which was all I was craving at that moment in time.

"It's funny, isn't it?" he continued, leaving his words hanging on a knife-edge.

"What is?"

"We spend all that time up in the Highlands, learning how to kill a man with our bare hands, how to make explosives out of some old wives' materials and here we are, trying to win a war by switching labels over."

I lightly snorted, realising that he was right.

"Perhaps they shouldn't have bothered with us at all," I whispered, keeping my voice low so that the others could not hear. "They could have sent a couple of schoolboys in our place."

"Not a chance," he said, quick as a flash. "Those

schoolboys would have more idea about what they were doing than us two buffoons."

We carried on looking at one another, our grins as wide as if we were looking in the mirror.

Nothing happened for a few moments, until, gradually, the scratching stopped. As if the nibs of the pens were slowly being withdrawn from the paper and placed back in satchels.

Before too long, the silence was perfect, as the huddle of five men stood shoulder to shoulder with one another in the centre of the room, slowly drawing weapons from their shoulders and preparing to withdraw.

I was slower to react than the others, taking grip of my sling and pulling the Sten gun into the front of my body. I gave it a gentle tap, enough to make sure that the magazine sat comfortably in the well, but not enough to accidentally discharge a round from the unpredictable weapon.

"Ready?" I breathed into the darkness, met with a smattering of nods and low grunts.

It was just as well that they were ready because, at that moment, there came a bark. A sharp, aggressive one, unlike all the other shouts that we had heard that evening. This one was authoritative and commanding, not like the jokes and chuckles that we had got used to.

This voice was angry about something, frustrated. And whatever it was that he had to be angry about, he was venting about it as he marched away from the station building and towards the isolated, rickety brick building in a railway siding.

In other words, he was coming straight towards us.

2

The smiles and grins, the ones that had looked so out of place on the faces of the men in the railway shed, had run away from them quicker than an overnight express train. Their faces, not miserable or downbeat, but totally emotionless, was all that I could see as I looked at each of them, one by one.

The sharp bark sounded again somewhere outside, as the man, incandescent about something, refused to let up in his onslaught. I could almost smell the stench of his breath, feel the saliva as it splashed angrily onto some poor soul's face, and I prayed a prayer of thankfulness that I wasn't on the end of such aggression. Never before had I heard someone with such a murderous tone than the man on that night.

I skipped my way to the main door of the shed, a big, eight-foot by twelve sliding piece of wood, presumably to allow trucks and other vehicles to back up to its entrance. Carefully, making certain of my footing with every step, I pulled myself closer to the door, until I was able to poke my head around and see outside.

I refrained for a moment or two, just to compose myself, and repay the debt of oxygen that was causing a shortness of breath. Clutching the door, I cleared my head of anything surplus to requirement. I forgot about what I had come to France to do, erased any memory of what we had been doing and certainly got rid of any remnants of triumph that was still clinging onto me.

"What is going on?" came a harsh, yet soft, whisper from behind me. The gentle tones of the Frenchman's dialect had always been met with warmth every time I heard them, no matter what the situation. Whenever any of them spoke, it felt almost as if their words were dancing around me on a breeze, and not breathed in a panic.

"Can you see what's going on, old fruit?" I could almost sense the other Frenchmen staring at one another as they tried to work out Mike's terminology, wondering what a piece of rotting fruit had to do with the situation. I hoped that they would ask him later.

I could say nothing, nor offer up any kind of intelligence, as I was yet to pluck up the courage to look round the door and see what kind of future lay ahead of us. I was praying for good fortune and that the voice was merely berating a young sentry for having one too many cigarettes while on duty. I figured that it was about time that we came across some good luck.

I flapped my arm around behind me wildly, trying to get them to quieten down and let me do my own thing. I was trying to blot out everything possible, the last thing that I needed was to feel like I was up in the dock defending myself. To their credit, they seemed to get the message pretty quickly.

I could sense them all behind me, their eyes boring into the back of my head until it burned, as I acted as their eyes to the wireless show that was playing out around us.

There was a tension in the air, one that was fragile, but I knew that each of them would remain calm. They had done so up until this point, as I could hear no one breathing heavily and sporadically as they panicked. We had all been caught in situations like this many times before, and to that point, we had all come out alive. There seemed no reason to assume that we wouldn't this time.

It was only as I pulled my head out into the night time air that I realised how much warmer it had been in the shed. My fingers still ached with cold, but my breath gave off a bigger cloud than it had done in the rickety old shed, and I pulled back momentarily, taken aback by it.

I peered out again, this time regulating my breathing and making sure I only exhaled through my nostrils, taking advantage of anything that may keep me hidden for just half a second longer.

I could just about make out the outline of the train station in the dark, a few lights here and there to aid me. Silhouetted figures kept interrupting the flow of light, as they all barrelled from their stations and to the man who was still barking orders.

There was just a handful, it seemed, that had responded to his calls, but I could not help but notice how a few others were dashing in opposite directions, obviously making with haste to posts that they had neglected to take at the start of their watch.

I focused on the barking figure, as he continued his slow march towards the shed. Even though I had not seen him, I would have guessed that he was an officer, and his peaked cap worn at a slight angle confirmed that.

Briefly, he stopped, and turned back towards the station, catching his face in a momentary outpouring of light as he did so.

He was still a distance away, but I got a decent look at the side of the man's face.

His nose was short, trimmed almost, and his whole face seemed to droop downwards, as if made of wax and had been subjected to a prolonged period in front of an open flame. His chin was non-existent, the bottom of his mouth almost seamlessly connecting to his neck. By all accounts, he was an ugly man, made uglier still by the ferocious growl that kept some of his men quivering as they ran.

He turned back towards the shed, as I realised that he seemed quite lopsided, as if one leg was far longer than the other. He limped towards the railway shed again, as men began to dot themselves about all around the area, taking themselves off to the water tower, the coal store and the tanker of petrol that we had failed to notice on our way in.

A clamp suddenly wrenched at my stomach, gripping it tightly and trying its utmost to flip inside me. My face strained as I tried to ignore its pain, but the panic that had suddenly taken hold of me was too much to forget.

I was suddenly very grateful that the others could not see my face as, although I knew they would feel the same inwardly, I did not want them to think any less of me just because my feelings had become apparent on my face.

The man barked again, his neck faintly wobbling in the dim orange glow of the station lights, before he became nothing more than a silhouette once more.

There were four or five soldiers crowded around him, each one of them with the stature of young men, obediently following at his heels.

As he barked though, they became more than young men, as they simultaneously swung their rifles from their shoulders, and made their weapons ready. The sound of weapons cocking, and rounds being chambered was unmistakable, the noise travelling further and clearer on account of the otherwise peaceful surroundings.

None of the men appeared as though they had done all that much training as, not only did it take them a long time to make their weapons ready, not one of them seemed to know what to do next.

One held his rifle with one hand, down by his side, while the others awkwardly held them across their bodies, as if this was their first ever time on a firing range.

I knew that the others behind me had already heard the bolts as they had clicked home and brought a round into the breech, but I had to make absolutely sure that they were ready.

I pulled my Sten gun from my shoulder and gently brought it round to the front of my body. I felt, rather than heard, the same leather slings as they brushed over the clothes of the men behind me. They were ready too.

"Everyone ready?" I whispered, looking back towards them, just to make sure. Even in the dim light I made out each head bobbing up and down in the affirmative. "Good."

"Are they still coming?" a voice breathed down the canal of my ear.

"Yes. About thirty metres away now."

The body turned away from me and I could hear him shuffling around as he relayed the news to the other figures waiting patiently behind me.

"We need to find a way out of this," breathed another voice from somewhere in the darkness.

Shooting our way out did not seem like this particular gentleman's cup of tea. It was quite fair, I thought, as it meant that the likelihood of being able to return to the railway shed for another go was increased, and there was no reason to believe that we had been spotted, yet.

The German officer stopped where he was, as he surveyed the scene and spoke to a tall soldier at his shoulder. I took the opportunity to duck backwards and hear what it was the others were whispering about.

"We could try and get over the tracks and into the field on the other side. It's in a slight depression so for the first few metres we would be hidden. We could crawl until we were confident that the mist would hide our withdrawal."

There was an uneasy silence, on all sides. The German officer was still stood where he had stopped, as his accomplice pointed out something to him on the far side of the station. His silhouetted body seemed almost as tense as mine.

"Hey, *Jean.* What do you think?" I almost forgot to acknowledge Mike as he appeared at my shoulder, I was that focused on committing the officer's face to my memory. I wanted to know everything that he had done, glean everything that he had learned. If I was about to fight this man, I wanted to know his weaknesses.

I looked down at Mike, who had seemed to shrink in recent weeks, his hair as long and wavy as ever, slicked back to perfection even on a night such as this. His eyes twinkled in the darkness, as his haste for a decision, which had made him one of the best pilots I had known, burned ferociously in his stomach.

"It's a risk," I rasped back to him, as I noticed the men behind him shuffling their feet like a worked-up bull.

"Johnny," he said, breaking into English for the first time in days. "Our whole time in this wretched country has been a risk. What harm can one more do?"

"I'm not sure I'd like to find out."

"So, what? You're going to sit in here and hope that *Herr Hund* out there isn't going to come in here?"

Herr Hund. I liked that.

I didn't take too much longer to think.

"Yeah, I know, Mike. I know. What's the plan then?"

One of the Frenchmen began to serenade me with his dulcet tones, quite out of kilter with the situation that we were in. Nevertheless, his voice was serious and sinister, as he explained the basic, but fraught plan of bolting from the shed and into the field on the other side of the railway line.

"All without being seen? Easy," I remarked, the sarcasm really only hitting home with Mike.

I watched as the other men scarpered to the far side of the shed, preparing to pull themselves through a meagre window and out into the night.

Disconnecting myself from them, I turned my attention back to the chinless German, who had slowly started to make his way to the railway shed once more. I could make out his voice now, which was not too dissimilar to his bark; gruff and aggressive with no hint of sympathy.

I turned quickly to the men stacked up on the far wall.

"Go. Now," I mouthed, as I leapt towards them myself.

3

The window through which the others had all disappeared was only chest height, but I still had an awful time of trying to pull myself through. I caught my shirt on something, and I winced as the ripping of the fabric tore through the whole shed.

Someone must have heard it, as a faceless figure appeared on the other side of the window and began hauling me through, just as I heard the first echoing voices begin to bounce off the inside of the shed.

A few torch beams began to flicker and flash around the crates, that all stood stock still and refused to give up our little secret. I was certain that one flashlight had just caught the sole of my shoe as it disappeared through the window.

There was little time to feel relief that I had made it that far, as I immediately began to prepare myself for what lay ahead. I had taken part in many a sports day sprint in my schooldays, but none was as perilous and life-threatening as the one that I had started to face down.

The other men had already dashed off, not wanting to loiter around any longer than was strictly necessary, and I realised that the faceless figure that had pulled me through the window was Mike, as his distinctive running figure made off into the darkness.

As his flailing arms began to make distance between us, I could just see another figure as he slid down the bank on the other side of the railway track. So far, so good. Four out of the five of us had made it to the ditch at the edge of the field.

Now, it was my turn.

I pushed off the wall with a gasp, my Sten flashing backwards and forwards in front of my eyes as I pumped my arms hard, taking as wide a stride as I possibly could without tearing a muscle.

Every thought that had plagued my mind vanished, as all I could think about was putting one foot down solidly in front of the other, and straining with all my might to see anything that might try to trip me up.

All of a sudden, I realised what it was the officer's accomplice had been pointing out to him as they had stood and admired the scene. A brilliant flash of light, quite unlike anything I had ever seen before suddenly erupted from behind me and just off to my right, before it steadied itself and ignited my path.

I sidestepped a hole that would have broken my

ankle, as I focused more than ever on making sure one foot landed in front of the other.

The giant torch held its gaze over me for a second longer, allowing the gunner to get his eye in and begin to release his fury.

The ground around me suddenly erupted, dirt and stone flicking up and chipping away at my skin. Then, as if the man could not control the weapon, rounds began sailing way above my head, the tracer rounds leaving a mark in the sky like a paintbrush.

After a few short bursts however and the man was able to bring the weapon under his control, and the deep, booming noise of the machine gun faded out, as the sounds of rounds far too close for comfort began to thud in all around me.

In desperation, as the rounds began to dance between my feet, I threw myself to the ground with a grunt, the wind being smacked from my lungs with a sledgehammer. I still carried on moving, crawling with earnest to get to the other side of the railway line.

I kept waiting for the inevitable sting of a round that had hit its target, the furious pain followed by the overwhelming disbelief. But it didn't come. So, I kept on crawling. The German kept on firing.

My shirt was ripped even more by the grating gravel upon which I crawled, and soon I felt the grit grinding into my skin and the wounds that subsequently opened. I felt large swathes of my skin being ripped from my body and great chunks of flesh simply falling away. But still, I knew I had to keep crawling.

I was trying my hardest to keep my profile as low as possible, simultaneously trying to make sure that I moved as quickly as I could. Up until that point my plan had worked, and I had no intentions of changing something that had been so successful.

A mouthful of dirt greeted me as I lifted my head, the machine gunner coming perilously close to severing my head from the rest of my body. But I felt instantly calmer, as I saw the flashes of light up ahead that told me that I had not been left behind. Quite the contrary, my companions were fighting for me.

Their bursts were short and sharp, but enough to divert the aim of the machine gunner away from me and onto their own heads, the earth around them spitting from left to right as he sprayed in their direction.

Their bursts of fire disappeared, before the gunner turned his attention back to me, repeating the whole process two or three times.

For the second time in as many minutes, I found myself being dragged, two pairs of hands this time had gripped my shirt and were pulling me towards them, the fabric tearing uncontrollably as they did so.

I fell down the bank head first, my fall cushioned by something soft and damp, the unmistakable stench of cow's muck telling me all that I needed to know. I had made it to the field.

"Almost as good as my dear mother's cooking!" Mike shouted, seeing what I had pasted around my mouth.

I did not know if it was the thought of eating the

muck that did it, or the exertion of crawling that had my chest screaming, but I emptied the contents of my stomach at my feet, much to the delight of a guffawing Mike.

"Any danger of you helping us out any time soon?" he shouted, the bellows of his lungs almost as loud as the popping of weapons that seemed to scream from every conceivable direction.

The rapport of weapons bounced off anything that was solid around the station, giving off the impression of ten times the guns that there actually were.

That didn't matter though, the machine gun that continued to rattle was dangerous, not to mention the small arms fire that was also beginning to chatter our way.

I pulled the Sten up and buried it into my shoulder firmly, just brushing the trigger at first before snapping away at it aggressively. Proudly, it bucked and kicked, flinging rounds to the enemy.

It made me feel better to fight back for a change, the taste of vomit almost leaving my mouth as a result. I made sure to keep my bursts short and sweet, levelling my weapon after each one to prevent the rounds from sailing high above the Germans' heads.

I finished firing off an entire thirty-two round magazine and dropped down further into the ditch, as I pulled the disjointed magazine from its well and fed in another one.

A momentary awe washed over my body, as I

stared at the winking weapons and the men's faces that flashed up behind them. It was quite a sight to behold, and I wondered if any of the pursuing Germans were having the same thoughts as I was.

Just as I fired off the next few rounds from my Sten, a morbid wail began to sound, drooling at first before gathering pace and confidence. I could not see anyone, but I pictured the sight of the man who had grabbed the handle of the siren and had begun to turn it enthusiastically, to warn everyone in the vicinity of the obvious attack.

But I was certain that I could hear something else in the background. Another siren, some distance away, rising and falling at different intervals to the one at the train station. Flustered, I looked across the line, the same, panic-stricken faces staring back at me.

If the Germans were calling for reinforcements in the town, then we may as well have turned the weapons on each other now.

There was an increase in the chattering of weapons, and I busied myself with discharging the last of my few precious rounds, but I could not ignore the fact that the distinctive bark of the German officer could be heard over all the commotion.

Something had got the Germans riled up too, more than a group of five infiltrators ever could.

The blinding light next to the machine gun suddenly stopped, the gunner keeping his finger depressed on the trigger for a second or two afterwards.

Darkness descended upon us all once again, with only a few pot-shots in the dark and the shouts of furious men to break up the silence.

We knew that they were edging their way towards us, and every bone in my body was urging me to turn and run through the muck-filled field. But something was stopping me from doing so.

There was a noise, a rumble, as if we had awoken some sort of sleeping giant, that was growing louder and more impatient until the ground quivered with such a ferocity that I thought the ground was about to open up.

"Air raid!" called one of the Frenchmen, a grin so broad that I wondered if he knew that their target was likely to be on his country's soil. As he shouted, the station lights were doused, and I could feel every muscle constrict as I prayed that they would pass us by.

The aircraft overhead had certainly brought us some good luck, but if my track record was anything to go by, then they had been briefed to bomb a well-fertilised field next to *École-Valentin's* only railway station.

"Shh!" I hushed across the line of shadows, holding my finger up to my lips desperately. The Germans knew where we were, but I didn't want to give them the opportunity to begin firing at the mystical noises that had emanated from somewhere behind the mound.

Row after row of planes continued to thunder

overhead, so loud and rich that I could not tell what kind of aircraft they were, never mind how many engines. I guessed that collectively, there was somewhere in the region of two hundred of them.

Mike began to fumble around in his satchel, as if searching for a family heirloom that had been entrusted to him personally. However, it wasn't a diamond necklace or precious letter, but something far more valuable to us.

Five, primed and ready Mills bombs, dropped to us a month or two before, were passed out along the line.

Mike and I had received extensive training on how to throw these things, in fact, we had been training for years in the St John's College first eleven cricket team, but the men beside us had received only verbal instruction. I prayed that they could remember it all, down to the last syllable.

German voices began to holler into the darkness, as they realised that the bombers' payload was not destined to fall on their heads that night. Instead, they were too busy themselves with hunting down the five men that had been seen a few moments before.

"Ready?" Mike rasped, receiving only quick, aggressive nods in return. "Okay then. Pins out."

We did as we were told, keeping the lever depressed to stop the striker from setting the thing off prematurely.

Mike began to count down from five, his left hand outstretched and clear to all of us. It seemed to take him an age before he got down to one, by which time I could hear the boots of the Germans over the gravel, as they cautiously closed the distance between us.

Mike's hand disappeared and, with an arcing, straight arm, I tossed my Mills bomb into the darkness, and ran.

4

I was beginning to think that maybe Mike and I had been together for too long. We had known each other for the best part of seven years now and, for the last three and a half, had spent almost every day together, fighting the Nazi war machine in some capacity.

But, over the last couple of months, where our relationship was required to intensify to an almost unfathomable degree, we found each other not only fighting together, but depending on one another. There was a distinct difference.

The difference was that, when we were under fire, there was no other person that I would rather trust but, take away that excitement, that utter exhilaration, and Mike's company was beginning to grate on me slightly.

"So, all these bombings…I know that we haven't really copped it where we are, but it's got me thinking…I suppose that someone, somewhere, is really feeling the fury of our bomber boys and…"

His voice continued to waffle on in much the same vein as it had done. His deep, commanding voice was as strong as ever, and far too early for my brain to comprehend on such an early morning.

It was easy for me to imagine my life without him, even just for a split second. Not so long ago it had become a reality, even if it was a fabricated divorce, just to further our war effort. I knew that had it been the case I would miss him tremendously, and I realised how much like a brother he had become.

I myself had never had a brother, but this was what I pictured it would be like. Frustrating, anger-inducing, yet loving and with a bond so durable that it could never break.

"…And what with the new bombs being developed all the time, it's only going to get worse…"

I looked at his face for a moment. It was hard to believe it as I stared at him but, had we been blood brothers, then we would likely have been twins. There was only a matter of months between the two of us in age, and yet, his muddied and rugged face spoke of a life of hardship, longevity.

It was only then that I realised that I had not looked in a mirror myself for a long while, and figured that there was a good possibility that I looked the same, perhaps even worse.

My face felt waxy and greasy as I wiped down the side of my cheek, half expecting a layer of green grime to rub off on my palm as I did so. I could feel the weight of my skin, heavy on my shoulders and drooping like an old man's, as I realised that the exhaustion within was quite quickly disseminating itself across my exterior.

It made me wonder for how much longer I could continue like this. I would surely need some kind of a break soon.

As we walked together, my mind became nothing but a sheet of white, a totally blank canvas. It was something that I had never thought possible before, with hours of rabid meanderings running around my mind, particularly in the summer sun of a South East England RAF base.

I began to long for the hours that I had wasted, sitting in a deckchair, just a hundred-yard sprint from my Hurricane, reading novel after novel instead of sleeping.

It was perhaps why I was so depleted of energy now, in comparison to Mike's buoyancy. He had been the squadron sleeper, the one whom you could rely on to be asleep at any given opportunity. In fact, he had probably spent more hours asleep in a deckchair, copy of *The Hotspur* stretched out across his face, than he had done in the cockpit of his Hurrie.

I let him continue to waffle on, knowing him all too well now to be aware that he would surely summarise his arguments in five minutes' time. I would tune my ears back in then and pretend that I had been carefully considering his every word.

His unrelenting energy levels, the never-ending preparing and voicing his thoughts, spurred my own mind to come up with a theory as to why he was like he was. Every time I ended up coming to the same conclusion, my weary mind not really wishing to partake in any more effort than it needed.

He needed to take his mind off something, someone. He had left behind a girl in *Tours*, one that he was exceptionally fond of and was willing to risk his life for. But, like everyone else in this war, he was called upon to make a sacrifice and, on the surface at least, he was all too happy to oblige. But, deep down, it was clear that he was torn, and that something else would have to occupy his affections until such a time that he could return.

And, for Mike, the quicker the war was over, the quicker he could get back to her, so he focused incessantly on bringing the war to a swift end.

"And with all the air raid sirens and whatnot, there can't really be that much of a justification…not from what I can see anyway…for why they're doing what they're doing…"

Had it not been for his mouth, motoring along at such a speed that even a sports car would be jealous, then the morning would have been quite peaceful, enjoyable even.

We were fortunate in that we now resided in a small village, dominated by farms, that meant we could pick a different route to walk every morning, and get lost in the early morning mist.

Except on that morning, as Mike refused to let up, the mist was thicker and greyer than usual, somehow heavier. It was noticeable as I breathed, as if the particles were somehow bigger and clung to the inside of my mouth causing a great thirst.

The smell of cordite and detonated ordnance was hardly surprising, considering the number of aircraft that we had heard roar overhead the night before.

It did not shock me that the topic of Mike's morning musings was the bombing, as the frequency of raids over our patch of France had undoubtedly risen in recent weeks.

Distant towns had borne the brunt of the force, with only the odd, stray, bomb falling onto *Besçancon,* with little consequence other than a disgruntled farmer.

"Are you listening, old fruit?"

"Hmm? Yes, of course. Carry on, Mike."

Unperturbed, he continued.

"Well, my theory is that they're hitting certain targets. And, if I'm correct, they'll be getting a damn sight closer over the next few weeks. I think we're going to have to shield ourselves with more than a blackout, if you know what I mean."

I grunted an acknowledgement which seemed good enough for him, as I began to think of all the poor inhabitants of the nearby towns that had suffered at the hands of our bombers.

I could not help but think of the fear that commandeered their rational minds the second that the sirens went, and the sheer terror of being able to do nothing but wait as the bombs fell all around them.

I tried desperately to put off the inevitable thought, but it soon got the better of me.

It made me think of my wife, and my young son.

They had perished at the explosion of a German bomb, quivering under the staircase of our house in Richmond, London.

Had it not been for me, they both would have survived, my stubborn and unrelenting belief that the Germans would never dare to bomb London enough to persuade them to stay.

There had been a safe haven, for the two of them, in a small country house in Norfolk, with Grace's parents, that would have been enough for them to stay away from the bombs. And, even if Hitler had decided to obliterate rural Norfolk, then at least I would have been too far away to not have to see the devastation of a ruined home, and the broken bodies of the two people that I loved most in the world.

"Are you sure you're listening?"

"Yes, of course I am. The bombs."

"Yes, quite. Well, as I said, I think I've had rather a good idea. A splendid one if I may say so. And I think we should relay it back to London."

The early morning sun, that was basking the fields all around in an orange glow, sparkled in his eyes as he spoke. He was clearly proud of what he was about to say but trying in earnest to keep a cool lid on things.

"Go on."

"Well, those bomber boys can barely hit a thing, can they? And not because they're not good, not as good as us fighter boys of course, but—"

"Cut to the chase, Mike."

He stopped walking, pulling my shoulders round so that I faced him head-on.

"What if we could do as much damage, perhaps more, than those bombers could do, in a single night?"

His eyes sparkled ferociously, as the tunnels of darkness that led down to them were momentarily illuminated with a passion that I had never seen before.

"In doing so, I reckon we could save hundreds, if not thousands of lives."

"How?"

"These towns are being targeted for a reason, correct? They all have something that helps the Germans to further their war effort. Ports, airfields, crossroads. But the towns around here don't have that, do they? So, what do they have?"

"I don't know."

"Factories! Industrial machinery! Raw materials! That's what they all have in common. Engines, steel, weapons, that's what their targets are. And I can guarantee you it's the same across France.

"My proposal is that we send small teams into these factories; five or so men a time, place some charges then get out. Watch the entire Nazi war machine come grinding to a halt because of a handful of men."

He beamed. I could muster no emotion, other than complete indifference. It was almost as if he had said nothing at all.

"What?" he said, agitated. "I thought it was a jolly good idea." He began skulking away, like a child and I immediately pulled myself together to rebuff his petulance.

"I never said it wasn't, Mike. I was just thinking it through, is all." I gripped his sleeve and pulled him round to face me. "It *is* a good idea, Mike. All I'm thinking is if it would work."

"Of course, it would."

"To pull something like that off would involve getting close to the target, literally within touching distance. The Germans don't leave these sorts of places out in the middle of the countryside like this," I announced, spreading my arms to illustrate the point.

"They protect them…If it was to work then it would work well, I think. But if it failed, and it is likely too, then it would fail spectacularly. There would be no coming back from a failed op like that one."

He pursed his lips as he looked towards the sun. I could see him chewing at the inside of his cheeks. He always did that when he was frustrated that someone else was talking sense.

"Look, why don't we think about it. We won't be able to stop the air raids straight away anyway. We'll keep it from London until we have a proper course of action. It's more likely to be approved that way and we can get proper resources."

He mulled things over, before turning back to return to the safehouse.

"I suppose that there is quite a lot to be getting on with, anyway. We have a busy few days before we could even begin to plan it."

"Exactly. In the meantime, maybe you can think about something else."

"Like what?"

"Like what we're going to have for breakfast."

5

I stopped twiddling the pipe around in my fingers, finally bringing it up to my face for the first time in five minutes. Giving it a slight tap, I made sure that the tobacco was packed properly and ready for a light.

As I pulled out the box of matches, I coyly checked the time on my wristwatch. Eleven thirty-seven. It was exactly the right time.

Carefully, I lit a match and held it to the end of the pipe, taking in a few puffs and trying not to choke myself to death. The pipe, a bland and unremarkable object was, I had been told, an expensive and popular brand, one that most Frenchmen would save for a long time to be able to afford.

So, it was reasonable for me to wonder why this particular pipe had been offered by one of the other members of the circuit, when I found myself in need of one. He had gone to great lengths to instruct me on how to use it, including not letting the flame dally for too long on one area, in case the rim of the pipe itself got burnt.

I let it hang from the corner of my mouth while it bubbled away, a few unwelcome mouthfuls of smoke reaching my lungs.

I tried to ignore the unfamiliar and rather unpleasant taste in my mouth by focusing on the man who had just got to the gate of the park.

I had first seen him a few minutes before, immediately knowing that he was my man. There was something about him that had made him stand out, not because of any garish features, but quite the opposite. He was so common and ordinary that he stood out like a sore thumb.

He was short, I guessed five foot four, maybe an inch or two more if I was to be generous, a slim frame but still bulging at the seams of his clothes. His spectacles made his face seem more pointed and sharper than it actually was and his eyes, skitting around all over the place, completed the image of a man who seemed completely out of his depth.

It was why, as he made his way over to me, that I was quite surprised that he did not call out and wave, giving the whole game away.

It was that fear, the game that had caused me many sleepless nights and even more irritated daytimes, that I changed our agreed plan, rather quickly.

I got up from the bench that I had found myself occupying and began to walk towards the opposite gated exit of the park. I walked neither so slowly that I appeared suspicious, nor fast enough that the man's little legs could not catch up, but I was far enough away for him to have to call out to me from behind.

"Eh, *pardon, Monsieur.*"

He looked at me, cigarette wobbling between his fingers, more out of nerves than anything else.

"Do you have a light?" His French was impeccable, so much so that I thought he could not possibly be my man. But, as he leant into my hand with flickering match, I heard the unmistakable sound of what I had been listening for, twice over.

"The weather in *Tours* is very similar at this time of year."

I stared at him, through his chunky spectacles, as he drew in a long breath of tobacco and turned his face to one side to expel the air, revealing a small scar along his jawline.

I sucked on my pipe before nodding almost indiscernibly and turning away, picking up such a pace that I could have been mistaken for running. The fact of the matter was that I didn't want to be around this fellow for any longer than was strictly necessary.

As I glided through the park, I sucked in far more air through the pipe than I perhaps ought to have done, coughing and spluttering my way to the perimeter gate.

Daring not to look behind, I felt confident that the man was following on behind me, his short stubby legs making it hard work to keep up with me, which was the desired effect. I did not want any potential onlookers to suppose that we were there for a reason, that our short conversation was nothing more than coincidental.

My pace slowed as my knee began to burn with fire, the stitches that had been etched into my skin still leaving their mark and preventing me from running with any real determination.

I exited the park and turned to my left, walking along the perimeter fence and, crossing the road, onto the pavement on the other side of the street. It was busier than I had expected it to be, with plenty of people skipping past one another and ducking into the road to allow a pram to get past unhindered.

There were few cars on the road, but instead one side was full of automobiles all parked and waiting for their owners. On my way into the park, I had not taken in how many there had been, and I felt my heart begin to flutter, my eyes skitting around, panicked.

I was looking for the car that I had arrived in, hoping that Mike was still ready and waiting at the wheel, but I could not see him anywhere.

Every bone in my body screamed at me to turn around and check if the man was still following me, simultaneously peering through some of the back windows in order to glance a look at the back of Mike's misshapen skull. But I knew I had to refrain.

As I came up with a contingency, walking around the block to pick up a newspaper and having a second attempt at trying to find Mike, I caught sight of a dark figure in one of the cars.

I threw the door open.

"What took you so long?"

"I thought you'd gone."

"It crossed my mind."

As I slammed the door of the Renault, Mike turned the engine over and crunched into gear, pulling away with an all-familiar whine.

He moved off slowly, holding back on the accelerator as if his foot had no more weight behind it than a dove's feather.

"Are they following us?" I asked, expectantly, knowing that it was not my job to turn in my seat and look behind us.

The reasoning for not looking behind was the same as to why I had planned to go and pick up a newspaper if I could not find Mike. We always had to remain aware of a third party in everything, not just the Germans, but also inquisitive Frenchmen who might question your presence without a purpose.

"Yeah. Two up. Passenger wearing thick spectacles."

"That's them."

We drove along in silence for a few minutes, taking random left and right turns to make sure that we hadn't picked up any kind of a tail whilst in the park. Finally, confident that we hadn't, Mike began to make his way to the safehouse properly. It was only then that either of us spoke.

"So, what do our friendly agents look like then?"

"I've only seen one."

"Alright, well what does he look like then? Good shape?"

"Not particularly."

"What makes you say that?"

I sighed heavily, as the smoke on my lungs began to make me feel quite lightheaded. The man had seemed short and quite dumpy, unathletic by all accounts and not the sort that one would typically assume would make a good agent. But London must have deemed him good enough, he would have been through all the same training as us after all.

"His French is good…every inch of him seems to scream unremarkable. Inconspicuous."

"So, what's the problem?"

"His feet."

"His feet? What's his feet got to with anything?"

"He's wearing a pair of Lobbs, for crying out loud."

"Lobbs?" Mike almost shouted, hitting the brakes harder than he should have done and almost sending the following car into the back of us. "As in the shoemaker?"

"As in one of London's most famous shoemakers, yes."

Mike muttered something under his breath that I couldn't quite catch, but I was fairly sure it would have made even one of the most seasoned sailors blush with embarrassment. We both sat, seething for a few more minutes, until Mike spoke again, this time with more apprehension in his voice than anger.

"Well, that wasn't there earlier."

"Let's hope they wave us both through," I said, observing the spontaneous checkpoint that had been set up. Two young privates stood next to a motorcycle, its machine gun facing back down the road towards us. Just behind them were two men in plain-clothes, leaning against the bonnet of a car, smoking.

"*Gestapo*," Mike stated, an observation that did not need making.

We passed the two soldiers, carefully, Mike even offering a quick flick of his hand as we drove past them. I never really knew what to do in such a situation. I had tried staring at them as we went past, waving as Mike had done, or staring dead ahead and not even acknowledging them, each option making me feel just as guilty as the last.

"No…" Mike groaned through gritted teeth as he let the accelerator come up for a second.

"What?"

"I hope that none of those soldiers like bespoke British footwear."

I turned around, forgetting everything that I had been taught.

Their vehicle was slowing up, as one soldier had stepped out in front of them, hand raised, the other manoeuvring around to the driver's window. Thankfully, the two *Gestapo* men had barely stirred. In fact, they seemed quite disinterested in the whole affair.

But that did nothing to quell the nerves that instantly stirred in my stomach. I replayed the scene in the park over and over, to see if I could picture any other man that had been there without good reason. Had someone spotted us? Had we been compromised?

But, if that had been the case then why only stop the one car, why not both? I began chewing on the end of the pipe, which had gone out a while ago, as I shook my brain to think of any possible connections that they may have had to us.

Mike did the same.

"They don't know where they are going, so they can't compromise the safehouse. They don't know our names, nor our faces. We can lay low for a while if it comes to it."

"He knows my face, Mike."

"It's quite a forgettable one, old fruit."

No amount of joking was going to make me feel any better. The man that I had seen, although he spoke perfect French, did not seem like the kind of man that would deal well in a situation such as this.

He appeared as quite weak and feeble, the kind of person that might break down in tears if asked too difficult a question. I could only pray that they had conjured up a solid cover story for where they were heading, and why. But it was unlikely seeing as they did not know where it was they were actually heading. They only had the name of a village. *Besançon.*

I prayed that would be enough to get them waved through.

"What now?" I asked, trying to break the silence that was doing nothing for the state of my mind.

Mike chewed on his lip as he thought for a moment, "Down here, at the end of the hill. We'll park up. There's a café. With any luck they'll stay on this road in the hope of finding us. We should be able to see them coming."

"Think that'll work?"

"Well, put it this way, when we hear gunshots then we'll know what's happened."

I looked at my feet in dejection, my face fallen. I had been quite looking forward to meeting someone else who had been sent by London, and now it seemed I would have to wait.

I looked up from my bland but comfortable footwear.

"Oh well, at least we won't have to find that chap a suitable pair of shoes."

Mike chuckled, as he looked across at me and shrugged. It was the only way that we could deal with such bad news. We were still alive, so we had to carry on as normal.

6

It felt quite normal to be back in a place that I had known for so long, the quaint shops where everyone had known my name and the benches where I had shared many a conversation with good friends and family.

Richmond had been my home for as long as I could remember, and it had been the last place that I had been able to be myself. No war, no lies, no death.

As I walked through the square, that was normally bustling with shuffling feet and chipper voices, I felt quite at peace. Everything seemed normal.

Not just normal for this war, but normal in every sense of the word. There was nothing that set it apart from its peacetime persona, everything was just as it was in the early spring of 1939.

Slowly, I picked up my pace, until I was charging along at quite a speed, my legs feeling as though I would soon outpace myself and end up flat on my face. There was nothing for me to be running towards, nor from, but I felt compelled to do so.

The bombs that had been a signature of my last time in Richmond were non-existent, there was nothing but the sound of my shoes clapping on the pavement as I thundered along. There was not even a sound of repeating steps from behind me as I had come to remember, it was just me. Mike was not alongside me this time and, in a way, I was glad. I had always regretted dragging him along with me.

I skidded to a halt at the end of a street, its sign now masked by a cloud of dust that had risen up over it. But I knew where I was, I had been there many times before.

There was nothing of the street, other than the road itself, with a pavement running down either side of it. But there were no houses, no other notable buildings, just an eerie dust. The cloud seemed to enshroud everything and envelop it all in its embrace. That was true of everything, apart from a small mound that I could see about halfway down and to the right of the street, where something had spilt onto the pavement, ruining the peace of the road.

"You can't go down there, son," said a voice, whose face suddenly filled my vision. He was a portly gentleman, with the air of a university professor but the personal hygiene of a vagabond. His face was dark and muddied, made darker still by the clouds that rolled around an unlit midnight sky.

I stared the Home Guard Captain down for as

long as I dared, as if inspecting his uniform and he mine. Both of us were covered in a layer of dust that made our uniforms a grey colour, altogether quite bland and neutral.

"But I live here. This is my home."

"No one lives here, son. You can't go down there," he repeated, just as monotone as before.

I shoved him to one side with fervour and great force, not caring what happened to him as I did so.

I was precarious as I moved, not wanting to cause any more damage to the street with my clapping footsteps that echoed out, as if I was in some sort of a cavern.

The streetlights were on, highlighting particles of dust as they flickered through the air, and were breathed into my lungs, making my throat itch.

The closer I got to the mound, the more that I could make out from the rubble. There were broken bits of furniture; a dressing table, a writing desk and a child's rocking cot. All were smashed and broken, splintered wood garnishing the mound sombrely.

Then, as I drew closer, a silent wind puffed out its cheeks to remove a particularly dense cloud of dust. The smell of detonated ordnance finally registered in my nostrils, a twisted stench of burning wood settling underneath and catching at the back of my throat.

The pale canvas of greying mist intensified, as if to angle a light onto the top of the rubble, drawing all my attention to it.

I resisted the temptation and turned to see what

had happened to the Home Guard man who had tried to stop me. But he had vanished. There was nothing but the dust, getting thicker, closing in.

I turned back to the mound, knowing full well that I would have to look at it sooner or later. It was not my first time here, and I was certain it would not be my last.

My hand quivered as I looked at them, as it always did. My lip starting to tremble in unison and the ground beneath me turning to liquid as I struggled to stand upright.

I crawled up the rubble, kicking bits of my home to the bottom of the pile, not caring an ounce for the things that I had built up in my life.

There, on the top of the mound were two bodies, lifeless ones. I was sobbing before I could even see their faces, which became obscured by the tears that rushed to fill my eyes.

Both faces were unblemished, but pale, their lifeless corpses seemingly the only thing untouched by the plethora of dust clouds that had formed all around. They both, had it not been for the icy cold finish to their skin, appeared to be fast asleep, quite at peace with everything and oblivious to the anguish that was billowing in my heart.

I was happy, in a sense, that that was how it was as, had it been the other way around, I would have been driven to torment at the pain that they had been in. I was grateful too for the merciful way in which they had perished. It had been quick and, if I was to believe the old tale, they would not have heard the bomb that had hit them.

It did not prevent the inevitable though and, as I let out a ghoulish wail, like that of a wounded animal, I felt quite dethatched from my own body, staring at the three figures, lying next to one another. I was desperate to stay there with them both, so that I would not have to experience the forthcoming anguish at being left alone.

"No no…Grace…My wife…Don't be gone. Henry, Henry, no!"

The whole scene was suddenly swallowed up in a black hole, as I found myself staring into the whites of a man's eyes, sad and concerned.

"Johnny. You're not there. You're here. With me." I watched as Mike stepped backwards from me warily, as if I was a grenade that had failed to detonate. A cigarette dangled from his mouth, that was burning dangerously close to his skin, as a sprinkling of ash fell to the floor as he sat down in the chair opposite me.

My body, still twitching and convulsing from the dream, was seeped in perspiration, as if I had just taken a full-body bath. I was cold and the tips of my fingers had turned a deep purple akin to a bruise.

"Here," he said, passing me a glass with a measure of liquid in it. I threw it down my neck in one go, thinking it would alleviate some of my thirst but instead doing nothing but irritate it. "Scotch," Mike remarked. "Andrew and Christopher brought it with them."

I let my mind settle for a moment as I tried to recall the faces of the two names. Then it clicked, Christopher had been the small, pointed man with large spectacles, his bespoke shoes regrettably thrown into the first fire we could find. Andrew, his tall and muscular accomplice, seemed the complete antithesis of his comrade.

"Those dreams of yours," Mike announced, lighting himself another cigarette flamboyantly and pointing it towards me in between his two fingers. "They're becoming more frequent."

"Why didn't you wake me sooner?" I begged, shuffling around and feeling more areas of my body doused in sweat.

"They're happening too much, old fruit."

"I can't help them. I wouldn't have them if I had a choice."

"Oh, I know, I know," he conceded graciously, as he realised that his manner had not been that much help to me. "And normally, I wouldn't mind. I mean it's only natural to...you know…After what happe—"

"I know."

"It's just that, everything you say…well, it's all in English. You need to be careful."

I wasn't sure how I was meant to respond, as I had no control over the content of my dreams nor the language in which they played out. Short of never sleeping ever again during this war, I could not see any other way to avoid such an occurrence.

My fingers still quivered as they had done in the

dream, and the sweats that had made the fibres of my clothes cling to my skin had refused to cease, as a bead dribbled down my spine.

At that moment, a small child tottered into the room, playfully, while I lit up one of my own cigarettes, to try and calm myself down.

"*Bonjour,* Georges," Mike uttered, as the boy looked at him before making his way over to me. He was only about six years old, but he had such a firm sense of what was going on in the world that he at times came across as someone three times his age.

He knew that his father was fighting to get the bad people out of his country, and that the four men who had recently come to live with him were helping him to do that.

His father, Jules Gambetta, followed him into the room.

"Not now, Georges. They are talking. They are important and they don't need your little ears taking the information away."

"It's alright," I said, sticking the cigarette in my mouth before lifting the child onto my knee.

"We were done anyway," Mike finished for me, as I looked into the child's wide eyes and smiled. My body warmed as he sat with me, a great deal of comfort from something so innocent emanating from his core.

We had spent hours together since we had first got to *Besançon,* largely in silence, just enjoying each other's company.

In a way, the company that I had from Georges filled me with an intense jealousy, particularly as the interactions that I had with him were ones that I never had the opportunity to share with my own son.

But that was through no fault of his own, and I enjoyed the time that I had with him.

I silently sucked in a mouthful of smoke, as I realised that my life in France had been characterised by a surrealism that was difficult to comprehend.

My life had become one of intense, long periods of boredom and inactivity, interrupted by brief moments of insanity and excitement, as close to death as a man could get.

Strangely enough, it was those moments, the ones where I was so close to death that I enjoyed the most, as it meant that the thoughts that plagued me in my quieter moments were all but forgotten, pushed to the back of my mind by the urgency that engulfed me.

"You have nightmares, *Jean?*" the boy suddenly asked, making me jump but also frown.

"Occasionally," I murmured, looking across at Mike, whose face was etched with worry. If the boy had heard the English language being called out in the night, it would only be a throwaway comment to a school teacher that would see us arrested.

"Me too," he replied, before proceeding to tell us both all about the episode up in some distant mountains, when he had lost his father, before being chased by some kind of demon.

I listened intently for, if I was to ignore him, I

knew full well that all I would be able to focus on would be the memories of my own nightmares.

I played along with the young boy, comparing notes on our nightmares and pretending that his were just as bad as mine. I could not run away from the fact, however, that the child must have heard *something*, and even that much was enough to make him complicit in what we were doing in *Besançon.*

Cautiously, Mike kept an eye on the two of us.

7

I smiled at Georges as he quivered in the bottom of the semi-waterlogged trench, his boots pulled on over the top of his pyjamas and a fraying blanket clamped tightly to his body by his father.

I knew that this was no kind of childhood, hauled from his bed in the dead of the night, to run to a trench at the bottom of the garden to shelter from falling bombs. But it was a reality that Georges had adapted to remarkably well. He was quite a stoic individual and I couldn't help but admire him.

The chill that I experienced as I watched him shivering made me feel closer to him, the smile that I received bringing me an element of warmth that I hoped I had given to him earlier on.

The trench itself was inadequate, to say the least. There were few shelters in this part of France, and the precious materials needed to manufacture proper shelters had been requisitioned by the

Germans some time ago. The few supplies that the Germans allowed to the civilian population of France were swallowed up, by the bigger towns and cities that were more appealing targets to the Allied bombers.

It was about seven feet deep, deep enough to encompass us all stood upright, but also enough to allow the water to seep up through the ground. It was why each of us was perched on a long wooden bench that Jules had put in to try and make our stay as comfortable as possible.

Above the parapet was a ragtag mixture of sheeted iron and planks of wood, designed to at least keep some of the blast and debris off us if we were to be attacked, with bags packed with dirt plugging the various holes.

It was, of course, useless if we were to take a direct hit, but it was better than becoming a fool and being caught out in the middle of the street with nowhere to go.

Had it not been for us, the boy and his father would not have even entertained the idea of having a shelter in their garden, opting instead to lose their lives in the comfort of their own home. But, at our insistence, they decided one should be built, even if it did mean that they were buried in their own garden.

I looked around at the others as they all huddled in the trench that was quickly becoming overcrowded. We had assured Jules that he would not need to extend the trench any further, it would not be long before we had found an alternative safehouse for our new comrades, Andrew and Christopher.

Andrew, his face in a constant blush it seemed, appeared calm and collected, slightly irritated that he was in a cold, damp trench, when he could have been tucked up in bed. The same went for Mike and to an extent I imagined that my own face too reflected this, as I longed to be warm again.

It was Christopher's face that concerned me the most, his eyes pointed to the sky as he rubbed at his face in panic at what was about to happen. He seemed frenetic and uncomfortable, as if he had never been caught up in an air raid before and had previously thought of them as a mythical story.

Something struck me as odd about him, as if he hadn't even known that a war was going on until about twenty minutes ago. It was a concern that would hamper me for days and greatly worry me every time that he stepped out of the front door.

The siren that bellowed all around, the one that had crudely awoken us from our slumber, continued to sound for as long as it dared, the whining incessant and grotesque. I prayed for it to cease, as it was causing me great discomfort and a pain was searing in the back of my brain on account of the noise.

Slowly, the operator of the sirens lost his bottle, and it began to wind down depressingly as the sound of aircraft engines shook the ground, small avalanches of dirt falling and being consumed by the boggy trench below.

The noise was unforgiving and as relentless as the siren had been, but infinitely more terrifying. I dared not to look at anyone else, out of a fear of giving away my own dread of what could happen.

The quaking ground intensified, until it felt as though the ground would open up and we would all be consumed by some sort of a black hole, which I began to pray for, as it meant we would be safe from the falling bombs.

The first wave of bombers though, soon passed overhead and, once the first row had rattled over us, we knew that we were not to be the targets tonight. It was a tense few minutes, hearing the bombers approach and then hearing the subsequent howl of their falling ordnance, relieved that it wasn't on your head, but equally sorrowful for the poor souls who were to be subjected to the onslaught.

"Not us," Mike breathed, confirming what we all knew.

"Not us," said Jules, giving his son an extra tight squeeze, one that I became immeasurably jealous of.

"If not *Besançon*, where?" Andrew queried.

"My guess would be the factories at *Sochaux*. They make parts for the Germans now. Big factory too. I reckon they're pumping stuff out for the Germans at a rate of knots."

There was no real reason why *Besançon* would have been the target of the Allies' bombs, but there was an apprehension all the same. *Besançon* was close to many of the industrial complexes in Eastern France, with many of the villagers supplying the factories with labour. It would be a valid target had Bomber Command wanted to cripple the workforce.

But that would throw up all kinds of questions of morality and kindness, as well as the fact that the Germans could call upon manpower from all across the continent. The real aim would be to knock out the machinery inside the factories. That would be a lot more complicated to replace than human lives.

"So, we are alright tonight?" Jules asked, wrapping his son in the blanket to try and keep him warm.

"For now, I would say so, yes," I murmured, reluctant to give him any certain assurances that could end up coming back to haunt me.

"Then I will take Georges back inside. He is very cold."

He was able to talk at a normal level, as the bombers had receded for the moment and were closing in on their target. The ground had ceased to shake and, had the presence of fear not been apparent, the whole landscape would have appeared almost peaceful, therapeutic.

"That's fine," started Mike, as Georges was bundled up in his father's arms lovingly. "But make sure you come back down here when the bombers make the return journey. They could drop their spares anywhere. I'd hate for it to be on your home."

"Thank you," Jules breathed, as he stepped from the trench and retreated down the garden, carrying his precious cargo.

A few seconds passed, before Christopher, the nervous-looking agent, spoke.

"Do you really think they would bomb us on their way home?"

"They wouldn't do it intentionally," I responded, looking to Mike. "But they have to get rid of all their ordnance if they want to make it home. They can't afford to waste precious fuel like that."

"It is better that those two are safe and come back down here," Mike confirmed, as Christopher began shuffling around on his perch.

"I'm going to go and watch what's happening," I announced, standing up. "Anyone else?"

"W-what do you mean, watch?" asked Christopher.

Mike dusted himself down, "We can see from up here into *Sochaux*, we can work out where they're targeting."

"Why would you want to do that?" chimed in Andrew, the other newcomer to our fold.

"Because we're working on a plan. Come on, we'll explain."

Mike and I left first, not really caring if the other two were to come with us, but they did, more to save face than out of a genuine desire to watch the destruction of a French town.

The sound of exploding bombs filled the sky almost immediately, nothing more than dull thuds from where we stood, but still a faint tremor vibrating through the landscape. The horizon was awash with oranges and dull glows, as incendiaries fell onto the town below and lit it up as if it was daylight.

So prominent were the lights that I could see the outline of silhouetted buildings as they defiantly stood tall to the falling bombs.

Within minutes, the whole horizon was burning a deep orange, as if the sun was rising earlier than planned, as the whole town of *Sochaux* was ablaze.

"How can anyone survive such an awful thing?" muttered Christopher, dejected.

"Because they have to," replied Mike, forcefully, perhaps slightly annoyed that a man who had not experienced the war to date was making such a comment.

"And you say you have a plan for this place?" Andrew asked, growing in confidence as that of his comrade waned significantly.

"Yes, you tell them, Mike."

He nodded, proud that he was going to be the one to deliver the good news, puffing his chest out as he spoke.

"The target down there isn't the civilian population, that's what some of them might think, but that is certainly not the case. Nor is the target even the Germans that are stationed there, if they were the target then our bombers would only ever bomb the coastlines…a shorter journey, it means less risk," he said, looking at the confused faces that stared at him.

"The targets are the factories. Tonight, my guess would be the automobile plant that is down there.

That seems to be the only one that they haven't tried yet. But, as you can probably see, they can't get close, and they're more likely to kill civilians than the machines."

"So, what is your plan?" Christopher asked, pushing his spectacles up his nose, never taking his eyes away from the glowing horizon.

"Our plan," Mike continued, "is to get inside the factory ourselves. Plant explosives on the most important machinery and get out. I can guarantee that after tonight all those machines will be back in working order by the end of the week. If we can get up close to them, we can make sure they're irreparable."

Neither of the two faces looked all that keen, as the orange reflected on their faces as the fires began to make ground in the town.

"A lot of people will die tonight. Through no fault of their own. They have to live there so that they can feed their families, but instead they will be killed by the bombs of the people meant to be liberating them. We could save a lot of lives if we could pull this off. But we would need your help. We wouldn't be able to do this alone."

They both shuffled around nervously, thinking over both the morality of the issue as well as their own desire for self-preservation. I looked to Andrew, who came across to me as the likelier of the two to concede that we were right. But I got nothing in response.

A few more minutes passed by in which we were

forced to watch the burning inferno that had started to rage, with the ongoing rumble of falling bombs. No one spoke, until the barrage was almost totally over.

Christopher, as wary and nervous as ever, was the only one to speak.

"Absolutely not. It wouldn't work. I am of course sorry for the people down there, but we are too precious. We could do a lot more to end their war if we just stay alive. If we try and do what you suggest, there is no way we would survive."

8

I knew that hell awaited us.

It wasn't a sense of happiness that I was drawing from my presence in the bombed-out remnants of *Clerval*, but a sense of dampened pride was apparent that I was able to get there, so that I could help.

We had left early, shortly after the all-clear had wailed out across the mourning landscape, as everyone had felt every single ground tremor and quake as if it had rocked their morale as much as it had their physical world.

My legs ached as they continued to pedal the ancient bicycle that had been sourced for us, towards the small village on the outskirts of *Sochaux*. For some unknown reason it had seemed more pertinent to allow Andrew and Christopher an easier journey, taking the newer, better oiled two-wheeled vehicles, and Mike and I the older variants.

Andrew rode straight-backed and confident, albeit

in a silence that was more than a little curious. Christopher on the other hand, wobbled about all over the place as he began gesticulating, almost forgetting that he was relying on his own balance to prevent himself from colliding with the ground.

"Remind me, would you, of why it is that we are heading towards this? I see no reason to involve ourselves in such matters. Surely the locals are able to sort out this kind of mess themselves."

I did not understand why, but neither of our two new comrades had wanted to head towards the destruction. In fact, it seemed as if they had both expected to have avoided the war altogether out here, only being called upon to pick up messages and provide weapons to cooped up resistors.

"How can any of the locals sort out that kind of mess?" Mike said, pointing towards a large cloud of depression that hung over the town like a demented star of Bethlehem. "There are no locals left."

There was a pause, that was crying out to be filled.

"We *are* the locals, now," I muttered, cycling as close as I dared to the man to make sure that he heard me. I was determined to make it the last time that he asked such a question of us.

Cycling towards the bombed-out towns and villages of Eastern France was not something that Mike or I had been trained to do, but it was something we felt compelled to do.

"We have to help," Mike stuttered, his throat

catching on something as he did so. "It is not something that we can just think about, we have to do it."

I noticed both of the newcomers looking to us, trying to read the emotions that were stained onto our faces. Similarly, Mike and I locked eyes with one another, as the connection that we shared deepened dramatically.

Tears had rushed to his eyes and, for a brief moment, he was standing before me, in his royal blue uniform, the new stripes on his sleeve denoting his freshly achieved rank, a Flying Officer.

The uniform, as everything else around us, was covered in a grey dust, as if the ash from a nearby volcano had erupted and spewed its contents all around us.

I pictured the bodies that were recovered from under several feet of rubble, most of them not even perishing as a result of the impact of a falling bomb, but because of a lack of oxygen. It was something that had always stuck with Mike, in particular.

Neither of us had wanted to help especially, we were quite able to have made some sort of suitable excuse to return back to our billets just outside of our airfield, but something had compelled us both to do it.

Wave after wave of enemy bomber had appeared overhead, a new, fresh drone coming every couple of minutes, as the fires from incendiaries took hold to guide the rest of the force in.

Entire streets had been flattened, schools and cinemas destroyed without prejudice. Homes lay ruined, in nothing more than piles of rubble, bodies strewn everywhere, with some sitting atop a pile of bricks that had once been a marital abode, a child—

I blocked out the nightmares that inevitably tried to come to the fore, the fear that if I was to think about it too much during my waking hours, then it would flow over into my unconscious times, when the screaming and cursing in a language foreign in this land could not be controlled.

Instead, I focused on what had been important to me on that night. There had been people there almost immediately, people there who were willing to venture out when it was still unsafe to do so, to make sure that the corpses of my loved ones were retrieved as soon as possible. There had been people there to help, and I needed to repay that favour, even if it was to people who had no knowledge of what had happened to me back in London.

Shortly after our correction of Christopher's mindset, we began to see the first victims of the previous night. Abandoning our bicycles, we started to walk the last half a mile or so to the epicentre of the destruction, offering only sympathetic looks to those people who were able to walk away from the devastation. It was the people unable to do so that needed our assistance the most.

People were walking around in a daze, quite as if they had recently been woken from some sort of hibernation that was taking its time to subside. Every person who staggered around the town did so as if they had been given new limbs, unsteadily stumbling like a newborn calf as it found its feet.

Some had managed to muster up a change of clothes, others had not. A few wore nothing more than their undergarments of nightwear, ripped and torn as they looked to the sky, awaiting a final flurry of bombs to finish off the job. One or two looked as if they were even praying for it to happen. I could not blame them in the slightest, they had lost everything but their lives and, in many ways, that made it even worse.

A man, dressed in the crisp black uniform of the police, stepped towards us, as he had done so on many a previous occasion. He was a good man, so we thought, a helpful and friendly fellow who had always been appreciative of our efforts to assist in any way that we could. Although, we were wary about how much he was working with the authorities, and so maintained the strictest cover possible in his presence.

"Ah, *Michel, Jean.* It is good to see you both here, with help also, I see."

"*Oui, Christophe et André,*" I said, as the two gripped the man's hand and shook it firmly.

"Can you believe that not a single bomb hit any of the factories around here? Almost all fell onto populated streets. A few, mercifully, landed in the fields around but there has been a great loss of life."

"I'm sorry that we could not be here sooner," I said, looking around at the recovery operation already underway.

"No matter, you are here now. That is more than we can say for some."

It was remarks such as this that had led to discussions between Mike and me about whether we could ask him for his help in harassing the Germans, and it was something that would no doubt come up again now that he had said it.

"Can I trust you to show your friends what to do?"

"Of course, *Philippe*."

"*Merci.*"

There was a noticeable increase in the crunch underfoot as we walked, chunks of debris and shrapnel unavoidable and threatening to roll an ankle or two as we stumbled along. It was impossible to look at what it was we were stepping on, as the unfathomable scale of desperation all around was enough to draw anyone's unrestricted attention.

Huge chunks of walls were missing, where deadly debris had become a weapon, catapulting itself into the nearest solid structure that it could find.

Houses were nothing more than a criss-cross of wooden beams and bricks, some retaining a vague structure that could be seen to have been a building once upon a time, while others were merely a mound, nothing but a pile of red brick and mortar.

I tripped on something, as I took in the ragged curtains that hung at glassless windows and realised that a hand had reached out to me and gripped my ankle. I sucked in a sharp breath of air, as I realised that the hand, itself covered in a faint layer of dust, was attached to a body, that had been covered with a blanket, but otherwise left where it had been found.

A small boy, no older than six or seven years of age, ran around, his eyes glued to the ground, leaping every now and then onto something that only he could see. As he scarpered across our feet, I noticed something moving in amongst the brick, a pair of large beady eyes keeping watch on his predator.

The boy continued to chase and provoke the rabbit from its various hiding places, trying to clamp it in his grasp to bring a faint ray of hope to his family.

"Over here, *Jean,*" I felt Mike breathe towards me, as the sobs of a desperate woman began to reach my ears.

She was kneeling on the floor looking through a suitcase of clothes and meagre possessions, her tears falling into the fabric of socks and skirts that could only have been hers. The clothes on her own back were ripped and torn, scorched in some places, and had she been of the right frame of mind, I was certain that she would have been encompassed by quite a chill.

She was muttering something under her breath, as beads of blood joined the mix of tears falling onto her possessions. Her face a mess of blood and dirt, she continued to scrabble around in the case, jumping as Mike gently touched her on the shoulder.

She looked at him, her eyes full of terror, speaking of a fear that her sanity would never be intact again.

"My keys," she muttered, repeating herself, "my keys. To my home. I cannot find them. I cannot find them."

"Here," Mike spoke softly, moving her hands away from the suitcase and encompassing her in an embrace. "We can help."

I began rummaging through her possessions, as she sobbed into Mike's shoulder uncontrollably. I moved what little possessions she had around, until I found what she had been looking for.

"Got it."

"Which house is yours, *Madame?* We can help you get your things."

She broke off the embrace with Mike, her body shaking as if possessed by a demon. She pointed, a tremulous, broken finger, before throwing herself back into Mike's arms.

I followed her instruction to the other side of the road.

"Mike," I stated, getting his attention and angling my head so that he would look in the direction that the woman had pointed. There was nothing there, apart from the back wall of a building that seemed to sway precariously in the early morning air.

The front of the house was non-existent, many of the materials used to build the house having disappeared into a crater somewhere below the house. It had been a direct hit. The front door was somewhere in amongst the pile of rubble, a small fire flickering away beneath the surface somehow.

"Right then. Let's see if we can get someone to patch you up first, shall we? We can come back later and sort out your house."

Mike guided her down the road, her head buried in his shoulder as they walked, the sobs not subsiding in the slightest as they retreated.

I looked towards Christopher and Andrew, who were dumbfounded, the same look on their faces that I had possessed on that night in London where everything had been ripped from me.

"Do something," I growled at them. "Help someone."

There were plenty of people for them to help and instantly Andrew sprang into action, his tall muscly frame standing taller and prouder than some of the remaining buildings.

Christopher, on the other hand, stood stock still, staring at a lifeless body of a young girl, dried blood having set around her chin as she had given up her final breath.

At first, I felt anger, which soon morphed into an overwhelming guilt, a deep sympathy for the man, as he stood without emotion over the body of the girl. It was not hard for me to place myself in his shoes.

I tripped and fell over the bricks as I staggered towards him, sending an avalanche of debris onto the street below.

I whipped my coat off and threw it over the girl. As if it had been holding him in some sort of trance, the unwavering stare of the girl that had encapsulated him vanished, and he stared at me with a hollow, harrowing look of a man more broken than the skeleton of the village that was left.

I knew it then, but did not need to say, but Christopher would now be one of the strongest proponents of our plan. Anything to stop the bombs from falling on children like that.

9

It was taking some getting used to, being back in the comfort of a warm home, with no threatening dust to stick at the back of one's throat. Every limb groaned as I pushed my back into the chair, wanting to take the strain off every part of my body possible. The burning pain in my limbs was constant, although not too debilitating, but the hours of crouching as I pulled bodies from devastated homes had really taken its toll on my exhausted body.

We had been out for a number of hours, so long that I had stopped keeping track, but I could barely remember waking up or approaching the bombed-out town, it had seemed so long ago. The only reason that we had stopped in our attempts was because we had been told to do so by the police, believing that everyone that could have been saved had been by then, anyone else who was still trapped under the rubble was likely to have perished already.

All four of us had scoffed down some hastily prepared food, some of which was not cooked through, which only added to the pains of my body. But now, I was able to sit down, in the comfort of an upholstered chair, that was positioned so that the occupant could glance out of the window, down the garden and look down on the spectacular sight of *Clerval*, now all the more spectacular for the wrong reasons.

As the sunset, its glistening glow a defiant symbol of hope for the remaining occupants, the dust and smoke that had continued to rise up was lit up, the silhouette of the few remaining buildings appearing to give up its final few breaths.

It did not take long, as my gaze remained unwavering and loyal to the town of *Clerval*, for my mind to wander to what the forthcoming night might bring. Within an hour or two, a perfect darkness would be gripping this part of France again, and the hooded figure of death would be rubbing his bony hands as he sought out another horde of victims.

As the clouds of ash darkened, a cloaked figure above the town was clearly visible to me, a shudder passing over my body as I forced myself to look away.

The bombers would be back again tonight, I thought. In fact, the men crewing the aircraft were probably already leaving the mess hall, having had what could potentially be their final meal. A thought crossed my mind, that I instantly loathed myself for considering.

I hoped that the bomb-aimers had their eyes in tonight. Anything to stop the suffering of the people of *Clerval* from dragging on any longer than it needed to. The sound of bombs screaming down all around you, without being hit, was a prospect that I could never desire. The feeling of utter helplessness and desperation was one that drove me to despair, even though the skies overhead remained clear, for the time being.

My eyes fell on the small mound of dirt that rose up higher than the rest of the garden, which was where we would crouch later on that night when the bombers returned. It was another prospect that I did not much care for, and which required more positive thoughts to counterbalance.

There was a chance, however small, that the bombers would not return for a second run. Maybe they had returned the night before to inform their superiors that they had hit their targets perfectly, and that the factory was out of action.

There was a possibility, more so a hope, that maybe the big knobs in Bomber Command had seen fit to stop such attritional raids on French lands, in the hope that morale would somehow be boosted.

But, if what our local friendly police officer, *Philippe*, had told us, then it was more than likely that they would be back. But I could hope. Especially in the light of what it was that we were going to do to help.

I took a sip of my drink and winced. It was a

necessary evil, and one that would help to settle the nerves that constantly felt like they were shortening. I placed the glass down on the table next to me, like we all had done, apart from Christopher, who had declined the luxury of a stiff drink that we had all felt drawn to.

My thoughts were interrupted by a flash of movement to the side, a blur of both light and shadow as someone moved very quickly in the room.

"*Jean!*" hollered the small boy as he bounded in towards me, throwing himself over the obstacle course of outstretched legs and mish-mash of chairs. "*Papa* said that I could spend a few minutes with you all before bed."

Jules appeared in the doorway, with a wearisome look on his face, as if he knew that his small son would get nothing but a few hours of rest before the sirens woke him from his slumber. It wouldn't be long before we were crouched in a hole together, whiling away the hours until the all-clear was sounded.

But there was a naivety that the boy possessed that helped me to cling onto a faint ray of hope that maybe, just maybe, tonight would be the night that the bombers didn't come.

I nodded to Jules to let him know that it was alright, before beaming at the boy and tensing in anticipation of the leap that he always executed with such precision. I braced myself as he clattered onto my knee, the toxins in my legs bellowing out in anger at the extra pressure that I had put my legs under.

"Come on then, *Georges*," I strained, as I tried my best to hide the exhaustion that seemed to have me in its vice. "What questions have you got for me tonight?"

The boy had learned quite quickly that I had experienced a life far different from his and his father's, and had a well-developed presence of mind for such a young child. As such, he would spend the last hour of his waking day routinely quizzing me on matters of life and death, what to do to rid his country of the German occupation and once even demanding to know what it was like to fly.

I had blushed at the question, ignoring the burning glare of Mike as I did. *Georges* knew nothing of my former life and did not know that he sat on the knee of a British fighter pilot, and that he was in the company of another just a few feet away. That was unless, by some freak opportunity, he had overheard my whimpering in the night, and had begun to piece together small bites of information until he could see a clearer picture.

But, in actual fact, his question had been nothing but an innocent inquisition into what it must be like to be a bird, one that was able to soar above the war and above the death, experiencing life from a godlike perspective.

I had answered with nothing but a short, 'I don't know,' but I knew the day would come when the boy would eventually find out.

"I think it's funny, *Jean*."

"What is, *Georges?*"

"That all of you have the same drink, most nights. At around the same time. Why is that?"

It was one of the rare occasions that Mike looked up and breathed sharply from his nose, mainly out of relief. He did not have as much time for the boy as I did, but he knew irony when he heard it.

"I suppose we must all get thirsty at around the same time."

"Then why not have some water?"

"This is better. It also helps us sleep."

"Does it get rid of the nightmares?" Mike's smirking ceased, as he took a slow, protracted sip.

"Yes. Sometimes."

"Can I have some?"

I chuckled as I looked up to *Jules,* mockingly asking for his approval, which was met with a smile and a shake of the head.

"I think that's a no, don't you? Next question."

Unperturbed by his failure, the young boy continued to look around the room, as if searching for inspiration for another question, determined that this one would catch me out once and for all.

"Him. Why hasn't he got one?"

"Ah," I muttered, looking to where the young boy was pointing. I racked my brain, trying desperately to think of an answer that would satisfy the boy's hunger for knowledge. It wasn't a case of moving him along to the next topic, I had tried that before, which had only served to make him even more curious.

I shot a glare to Mike, screaming for assistance and blaming him for not helping me out.

"He's not thirsty," Mike spluttered, as his latest sip caught him at the back of the throat. It was a terrible answer, but worth a try.

Christopher continued to sit as he had done for the last hour or so, his legs crossed and pulled up tightly, his barely existent chin tucked into his chest and his spectacles twirling away in between his fingers.

His nose seemed less pointed than it had done before, his cheekbones disappearing under a thicker layer of skin. It was as if what had happened down in *Clerval* had served to refine him slightly, to sand down the rough edges of his character. If that was the case, then he was taking time to adjust, as he had barely said a word all evening.

"What's the matter with him?" the boy questioned, tilting his head to one side as if trying to understand Christopher a bit better.

"Nothing. He's thinking, just like you. Except he's doing it inside his head."

"No. He is different to you. He's—"

Jules swept across the room as elegantly as a duck landing on a glassy lake, simultaneously scooping his son up and also giving me an apologetic look.

"Right, that's enough of that. Come on, time for bed."

Jules was not angry, but there was an obvious tone of frustration in his voice. It was good, I had told him before, to let the boy think aloud, to ask all the questions that he had pent up within him. But that had been one of the occasions where he had wished that he had followed his own gut feeling and ignored mine.

Unintentionally, I caught Mike's eye, as he slowly but firmly placed his glass on the table next to him. His lips were pursed, and I could tell that the pressure of his blood was beginning to rise.

I broke away from his gaze, as his face told me all that I needed.

If the young boy can spot something is up, so could the Germans.

I turned my attention away from Christopher, as worrying about the demeanour of a man that had witnessed the effects of a bombing raid for the first time would get us nowhere. Although it would have to be something to consider seriously before too long.

Instead, I was drawn to Andrew, his permanently red cheeks not reddening in the slightest at what had gone on. It was as if he had heard it a thousand times before.

His shoulders were pushed back into the chair he occupied; his chest flared outwards as if he was preparing to take a volley of flaming arrows to his trunk. My heart rate settled as I thought about him and took a great deal of comfort.

Andrew seemed more switched on than his comrade, more aware of what was going on around him and what was going to be required. If I learnt anything as Jules' footsteps quickly retreated up the staircase, it was that Andrew was going to step up to whatever task we lay before him.

The same could not be said for Christopher, who was quickly becoming more of a liability than any kind of assistance. It was a worry that I could have done without altogether.

10

Both Andrew and Christopher had been around long enough now to be getting stuck in good and proper to the work that Mike and I had started. As such, it was decided that the two of them should begin to join us on our transmissions, to begin learning what it was like to send in hostile territory. All too often we had heard of new agents, who had been trained for months on transmitting, only to fall foul of the totally different environment of an occupied country.

All four of us heading out for the sake of one transmission was far too dangerous and, as Christopher seemed the more volatile of the two, it was decided that Mike would be the one to take him out.

So, as I waited for a final message from London, Andrew was crouched not too far away, peering down the street of our safehouse, keeping watch for any Germans that did not seem to have a purpose.

We had learnt how to spot them by now; if they

were walking slightly slower than the average German, or if they looked around too often, it was guaranteed to be a radio finder. There would be a waiting truck around the next street corner, which would come haring down to take us all to the nearest police cell for interrogation.

Although he wasn't listening in to the transmission, or really doing anything directly involved with the wireless set, it was good for Andrew to get out, and to learn the kind of precautions he would have to take once he was out on his own. I was certain too that it had been good for him to get away from Christopher, as it was clear that the millstone he was continuously carrying around was weighing heavy on his mind.

I was straining hard to hear the dits and dahs as they came through but, despite that, I still missed the first few digits as they squeaked into my headset.

I began scribbling furiously, trying my best to decode as I went.

Hello Fortunae Circuit...

I abandoned my attempts to go any further, deciding that the integrity of the message was far more important than knowing what the message had to say straight away.

It had always comforted me though, to hear those first few coded words, '*Hello, Fortunae.*'

It meant that we weren't alone. There was someone, somewhere, perhaps with a big map of France, who was waiting for us to contact them, poised with a message meant only for our ears.

Fortunae also brought me great comfort and I still recalled when Mike and I had been assigned the name as if it was yesterday. There was a sense of irony at being labelled something that was meant to bring good luck, but it nonetheless made me feel like I had a slight advantage over any other name.

Then, quite suddenly, as my finger hovered over an empty piece of paper, anticipating another load of dits and dahs, there was silence over the headset. That was that. London had switched off and we were now alone again.

I flicked the headset from my head and started to let my mind whirr and decode the message. I had done it so many times before now that it was almost like reading a slightly long-winded newspaper article to me. It was hoped that it would take the Germans days to read, by which time the information would be out of date.

Andrew began to watch me as I packed everything away into the case, making sure that the coils were neatly tucked away and the headset carefully folded.

"Well?" he asked, surreptitiously, gliding towards me as if I was now in possession of the greatest secret of the war.

"Not here," I stated, defiantly. "Never here. When we get back." He looked at me with disappointment etched on his face. "It is safer to. Safer for Magheritte."

He looked at me with a puzzled look on his face.

I refused to answer his silent question, instead busying myself with the final few things on the wireless set, memorising the transmission, before burning the paper under the flame of the paraffin lamp.

Magheritte, the lady whose attic we occupied, had been a great help to us already in the few short months that we had been around *Besçancon*, the mother-in-law of Jules and Georges' grandmother. We knew that we could trust her.

But that wasn't the reason why we never spoke a single syllable to do with our work in her house. It was to do with the fact that we knew what the Germans would do to people like her if they ever found out. She would be tortured and, although she was a lady with great courage and defiance, if she knew anything, she would tell the Germans immediately. Anything to stop the thin pins from being driven up and under her fingernails.

She knew the risks and yet was still prepared to have us in her home.

"Tell me about Christophe," I enquired, as I watched the paper curl and smoke above the flame.

"What about him?" he asked, shuffling around on his feet slightly and returning to the small opening that allowed him to look down on the street below us.

"Everything. Why is he the way that he is?"

The words 'I don't know what you mean' were hanging on his lips, but he knew immediately that it was a futile defence. Everyone had seen it, even the young Georges had called him out on it.

He was nervous and I didn't blame him. The two of them would have trained together right from the start, up until the point where they had both been parachuted into France.

"You are good, André. I can see that. So can Mike. But Christophe? Not so much."

He rubbed at his eyes, that had puffed up to the size of cricket balls, and were just as red, before clearing his throat apprehensively.

"He is a conscientious objector," he said, locking eyes with me and seeing my utter horror. "*Was* a conscientious objector. He doesn't believe in the war."

I went to ask him an obvious question, but he put up his hand to continue.

"He was a firefighter for a while, but then the whole question of his father's family came up."

"His father's family?"

"They are all Jewish. They left France some time ago for a better life in Britain. A year or so ago he started reading about the Nazi racial policies. And then, of course, the rumours came through about these camps that they put them in.

"It was then that he turned, apparently. That there is a case for someone to be a part of a wartime machine to defend others. It does mean that he is always looking for ways to harm the Germans without actually putting any of them in the ground."

"He won't get on with Mike all too well then."

"He didn't get on with many others at Arisaig either I can tell you. Including me."

The mere mention of the name brought back overwhelming memories of difficulty yet triumph. Arisaig had been the first place that Mike and I had first got a sense of what we were letting ourselves in for, and the months of training that had followed were almost too much to bear.

"He wasn't all too good in training, I feel like I should warn you."

"How do you mean?"

"Weapons. Explosives. Everyone else took to them like a duck to water. Christophe was something of a brick. Learning Morse code takes time, but I doubt if he even knows three letters now. The only thing he seemed any good at was the French culture side of things, and that was only because he has French blood in him."

It wasn't exactly the full-blooded endorsement that I had been hoping for. In fact, it was painting such a poor picture of the fellow that I felt inclined to go back and dismiss him from his duties.

As I mulled everything over, I began to feel more isolated, far lonelier than I had done just five minutes before. I had always enjoyed my little chats with London, however formal and brief they were, as it made me feel like I had a companion, a big brother of sorts, always watching out for me and ready to step in.

But, after the revelations of Andrew, I felt like I had been betrayed by London. I quite quickly became convinced that there was someone, in the depths of the busy corridors and offices, that wanted both Mike and me dead, and the best way to do that was to send in someone so inept and unrounded that he would give us up in a matter of weeks.

The thought even popped into my head about whether we wanted to win the war at all with people like Christopher being involved in such a dangerous environment.

"Right," I muttered, my throat gurgling as I tried to buy myself some time and think through what to say next. In truth, there wasn't really anything I could say, apart from asking the inevitable question that I did not really want to hear an answer to.

"How did he pass training then? It wasn't as if they were averse to cutting people. Why have they sent him?"

I waited for the answer that he was a well-connected public schoolboy, wanting to get his teeth into a sense of danger, before getting his mates blown up and collecting his handful of medals.

"Well, he is good at one thing. Just not the practical things. I think it is why I was sent here with him. I did well in training, but I'm not great with people."

"Why does that matter?"

Seemingly, he ignored me and carried on regardless, "He can empathise with people. He understands their situations and listens to them. I, on the other hand, just want to get stuck in. Adding other people into the mix can make things messy, stops things from working out."

"He didn't seem to empathise with the people down in *Clerval* earlier today."

"Oh, he did. He is a sensitive sort, the kind that takes time to process what we saw. He will be deeply affected by it; he'll be thinking about it non-stop for days. But it will mean that now it has stuck with him, he'll want nothing more than to see an end to it immediately."

"But what good will his empathy do for us? We needed a fighter, not a priest."

"It could do a great deal more than you could ever imagine, trust me," he said, his eyes deviously flicking out towards the street below so that he didn't have to hold eye contact with me. "I've seen him able to persuade people to do things that you never thought possible, all because he seems to have a way with people."

"Right," I muttered, with nothing else to say, simply allowing my thoughts to continue to rampage around my head.

I flicked the lamp down so that the hissing flame eventually went out, before heaving up the suitcase to my side.

I still did not feel all that confident having a man such as Christopher on my side, as I had quickly realised that he was going to take a lot of managing to be able to get the best out of him, or to get anything at all.

Guiltily, I thought it best to hide all of this from Mike, as I knew that his thoughts would be compulsive and irrational, and it wouldn't be totally impossible that Mike would somehow get him removed from the circuit.

I needed to trust Andrew's judgement, and that was exactly what I was leaning on as I turned to step back down the attic ladder and into Magheritte's home.

"Come on then, let's get back."

11

The pace of life as an agent in France was at times so startlingly slow that it seemed like months could pass without anything really noteworthy happening. But it would be pricked from time to time, where something would happen, a new piece of intelligence would come to light, that would mean that everything would sprint along at such a pace that it was difficult to keep up.

Once Andrew and I had made it back to Jules' home, that night felt like such a moment. My thoughts were sprinting, harder and faster than ever before, and as such it felt like hours had passed before I could even speak.

The others knew that whatever information we had would lead to one of two emotions; excitement or disappointment. Because of that, they were eager to find out what we had learned. It was three in the morning, but each of them had stayed up, eyes wider than if they had just woken up.

As Andrew and I entered the room, the three of them shuffled in their chairs, turning their bodies to face us. They were ready for whatever it was that we were about to tell them.

I thought of the small boy Georges, the only occupant of the house who was not in the room with us, and pictured him fast asleep, curled up in a ball until morning. I wondered whether or not he would ever know what went on when he went to bed, the five men downstairs plotting and coming up with devious ways to disrupt the Germans.

I hoped that one day his father would tell him of us, and that he would look back on the time with pride, that his father had played an integral part in trying to defeat the Germans. To do that, Jules would need to survive, which was why I had been keen to distance him from any of our conversations. But, at his insistence, he almost always joined us, silently.

The tension of the situation was such that even Christopher had turned to look at us as we entered the room, his stupor broken by the hold of the impending news. I looked him up and down, far more worried about him and his abilities since Andrew's revelation than I had been before. There was a sympathetic look on my face, one that spoke of the foresight that this man was going to die in this world, unless I could look after him effectively.

Gradually, my eyes met with the other two pairs of eyes that were staring at me; Jules first, then Mike.

As soon as I looked at Mike, I felt compelled to look away once again, a wave of shame and awkwardness descending on me in equal measure. He knew that something was up. He could tell that I knew something that he didn't.

Slowly, forlornly, he removed his eyes from mine and instead looked towards the clammy face of Christopher. There was no point trying to hide anything from Mike, we had been together for so long that we knew when one another needed to go to the toilet, hiding something of that magnitude was never going to hold for that long. I had hoped that it would have lasted ever so slightly longer than it had done, though.

"Right, well, I suppose there is not much reason for delay. Then we can all get to bed."

I tried to laugh weakly, which was only met with even weaker responses from those sitting down.

I cleared my throat in anticipation, as I took a rickety old wooden seat next to the table and turned to face my comrades. My throat had dried rapidly, the moisture sucked from it and instead distributed to my palms, which I wiped down the sides of my legs firmly. For some reason, I was nervous, overwhelmingly so.

"London received our message about the bombings, and our idea." Everyone held their breath, including me, despite knowing what was coming next. "As such, they have seen fit to stop the bombing runs over *Sochaux* for the time being."

A great exhale of breath was felt rather than heard in the room, and I thought for a moment that Christopher was going to get up and hug me. Tears had flooded his eyes as he bit down on a clenched knuckle, presumably to prevent himself from sobbing uncontrollably.

My own words tripped me up as I thought what they meant for the people who lived there, particularly the remaining occupants of *Clerval.* They would be granted a reprieve, a period of time to be able to restore some sort of normality, if it was ever going to be possible again.

But they would not know of the news, and why it was happening. Only that the raids had stopped. I wanted nothing more than to run as fast as I could to tell them all, so that they could sleep in their beds for the time being, without having one ear open to listen for the sounds of the wailing sirens, or the drone of engines overhead.

"For the time being?" Mike said, interrupting my thoughts.

"Yes. Unfortunately, they haven't suspended the raids indefinitely. They have given us four weeks. If, after that time we haven't been successful, the raids will begin again."

We all took a few seconds to process this latest bit

of information, some taking longer than others for it to truly sink in.

"Well, I'm sure those lazy beggars in Bomber Command will be happy for a few nights off at least."

Mike began to chuckle, as well as a smattering of other polite titters from around the room. I knew that he was only speaking in jest, but I couldn't help but harbour a slight frustration with him, especially as we both knew that those boys would simply be sent to batter someone else instead. Despite the rivalry between those in bombers and those who, like Mike and me, had flown fighters, there was a united desire for no one to get shot down.

"A few nights off is more than we ever seem to get," Andrew said, shuffling forward in his seat, his eyes twinkling with excitement.

"You speak for yourself!" Mike chimed, triumphant that he finally had a playmate to bounce off. "We've been here a lot longer than you two!"

The chuckles intensified, and I was even certain that a slight sharp exhalation of air passed through even Christopher's nostrils as he listened to the two of them going back and forth.

"Yes, of course, you have. But we'll be here a lot longer after you've managed to get yourself killed!"

I wondered for a moment if Andrew had overstepped the mark, but a half-second pause was all the time that I had to ponder the thought before Mike burst out into a great roar of laughter, enough to threaten waking up the entire neighbourhood.

Andrew and Mike became the biggest contributors to the noise, but in truth, we all let out a few relief-ridden laughs that seemed to ease us all. That was until Jules decided to speak, with authority and over the childish chuckles.

"Four weeks. It is not long for what you are proposing."

The laughing stopped almost immediately. He was right. Our plan involved lengthy periods of observation and note-taking, and that was before we even got into the nitty-gritty of what explosives and weapons we might need for the operation.

We did not have too many stores to call upon, everything would need to be arranged with London and dropped in. We would need a firm plan, with a shopping list, in place by the end of the week.

It was a sobering thought, and one that was shared with everyone in the room. There would be no more time for chuckling and messing around, we would need to be as focused as ever.

"We will have to start preparations right away then," Mike offered, looking at each of us in turn. "We can't afford to lose a single hour."

"Maybe we can sacrifice a few so that I could get some sleep?" I asked, my mouth conveniently drawing wide as I yawned.

"Makes sense. We can start in the morning. Good-night, gents."

"Wait," I blurted. "There's one more thing."

Mike repositioned his buttocks in the chair that he

had already started to rise from. Four panicked faces glared back at me, each one of them knowing that the appendices to my message were hardly going to be full of good news and joy.

I tried to think through what it was I was going to say, my words jumbling themselves up in my head to the point where I became convinced they would come out as nothing more than a garbling mess. It was as if my mind already knew that the next few weeks would run away from me at the speed of light and it was feeling the need to make a protest against it immediately.

"London have received intelligence about someone turning up in *Besançon*. An SS officer."

"So? We've put up with them before, I'm sure we can do it again."

"They wouldn't have mentioned it if they weren't worried, Mike."

"Do they know who it is?" asked Christopher, his voice trembling slightly.

"Yes. A man called Franz Mökhen. He has been tasked with keeping the resistance activity in this area at bay."

There were no jokes or snide remarks this time, only a deadly serious sea of deadpan and concerned faces. This man was dangerous enough for London to have on their radar, which meant we would have to take him with an equal dose of sincerity.

"Do you suppose he was the one that we encountered at the train station a few weeks ago? He seemed like he would have a name that sounds like that, Murky did you say his name was?"

"Mökhen."

"Murky, same thing."

"It could have been him. Hard to tell though without knowing what he looked like. Either way, we need to be careful. If he has a reputation back in London, then we know that he must be dangerous. We can't afford to make mistakes with someone like him around, can we?"

"True. But when we've been given a time frame like we have; we're going to need to cut some corners somewhere along the line."

Mike seemed impatient, which was worrying me. It was true that four weeks was not all that long to do everything that we might have hoped, but it was still long enough to think through our decisions and make informed choices. There was no need to needlessly end up in the clutches of the SS officer Murky.

"Mökhen. Mökhen. I've heard that name before. Where have I heard that name before?" Andrew asked, his reddened cheeks puffing out as he struggled to recall something from the depths of his memory.

I glared at him, willing him to remember, as our lives could well end up depending on it. I could feel Mike's eyes similarly pestering him to recall where he heard the name, as I prayed that it was as a result of an incredible incompetence that the man had come to London's attention.

"Mökhen. I've heard of him," Jules piped up, taking us all by surprise.

"And?"

"There are rumours about him. Not very nice rumours. He was in command of an SS battalion when they had the French and British armies trapped in the north."

"Dunkirk?"

"Yes. He captured large numbers of soldiers. French and British. They surrendered to him. He rounded them up and executed them."

There was a silence for a moment or two.

"How many?" asked Andrew.

"Does it matter? If the rumours are true, then we should be very concerned that this man is around. There are no rules in the war that he is fighting. That is dangerous enough."

We sat, shocked for a moment and I subconsciously looked over my shoulder as if expecting to see the officer from the train station standing over me, licking his lips at the thought of another execution.

I looked at my watch; four-thirty. Jules caught sight of me doing so.

"If that is everything, I think we should retire. Not long to go until sunrise."

"There was one other thing," I said, as panic set in once again. "I think a lot rests on this operation."

"What makes you say that?"

"Because something was sent in the transmission, after we had both signed off."

"Why would they do that? What did it say?"

"*See it done*."

Mike paused for a moment.

"No pressure then."

12

There was a particular art to following someone, that I always remained conscious of every time that I found myself hot on somebody's heels. I had spent months training on how to put an effective tail on someone and what to do if you somehow thought they had noticed you.

I had spent hours poring over books and articles on how best to track someone but, the place that I really learnt how to follow someone well was by being followed myself. It made me aware of all the things that were done wrong, the various ways that the prey could try and escape and ways around that, and minute details such as how close I could reasonably get without causing too much suspicion.

I must have spent days wandering around various towns and villages in Britain, having had just minutes to survey a map of the local area. The key was to work out where all the dead ends were because, if you found yourself down one of those, then you would need to be prepared to fight your way out of the situation.

For the tail though, the key was always having a reason, an excuse, as to why you were where you were. It seemed simple enough when you were tailing someone through the local high street, you could look through hundreds of shop windows and not arouse any suspicion. The real test came when the shop windows were non-existent, and it became near on impossible if someone was making their way across a country track or field.

These thoughts were constantly whirring through my mind, as I continuously prepared to give an account of myself if I was to be challenged by the man that I was watching, or a local police officer or inquisitive soldier. I also ensured that I did not keep my eyes boring into the back of my target's head, that was unnatural and, if he was to turn around, he would notice me immediately.

It had not stopped me from noticing however that he had a rather odd walk. He seemed to limp to one side for a few paces, before limping on the other side, quite as if the pain in his legs could not quite make up their mind as to where to settle. It added another complication into the mix for me though, it meant that he was walking slower than the average person, meaning that I had to walk just as slow, which threatened to give me away with every pace.

All in all, though, the last fifteen minutes or so had

largely been a success. We had tailed the man from the factory as he clocked off for the evening, and he was still blissfully unaware that he was being followed.

I took it as a good sign, that he was still nonchalant in the way that he walked as, if he was jittery and jumpy, constantly looking over his shoulder expecting someone to follow him, then the whole operation might have been called off there and then. We needed a cool-headed man for this job and, so far, he was fitting the bill.

The man slowed up and crossed the road. Unconsciously, I slowed also, but refrained from following him to the other side of the road, as he had stopped at a door to one of the houses.

I willed the door to open before I got level with him, as the second that I had passed the door, I would not be looking back. I had no reason to and therefore it was too dangerous.

When I was only a few feet away from drawing level with the door, it squeaked open, a young, pretty face there to greet the man. He wasted no time in stepping into the house, before he pressed his lips to hers and closed the door slowly behind them. Their lips were still locked together a few seconds later when I drew level with the door and caught a dying glimpse of the two of them.

Frustrated ever so slightly by the inconclusive nature of my work, I paced off to the end of the street, planning to round the block and make a second pass, this time with a newspaper under my arm. I would have had to have been incredibly fortunate to see him emerging from the house at the exact time that I passed, but it was worth a try, something might jump out at me.

My footsteps began to echo off the walls of the terraced houses, some with glass still in panes, others without, and I noticed that there was another set of steps, completely out of sync with my own, that were gradually coming towards me.

I pulled my pipe from my pocket, already pre-packed and waiting for its curtain call and placed it in my mouth, just as the footsteps drew level with mine. I stuck my arm out.

"*Pardon, monsieur.* Do you have a light?" I let him light my pipe, giving it several puffs, billowing smoke everywhere, before I loudly pretended that I hadn't noticed who it was.

"Ah! Christophe! How have you been, my friend?"

We shook hands, as Christopher took another match and pressed it to the tip of the cigarette that hung limply from his lips. It seemed to epitomise him no end, the way his cigarette dangled, just like his arms did from his side and the way that his shoulders were hunched forwards. It was as if he had no real drive, no desire to want to stand tall and proud, and that he was happy just the way that he was.

"So," he said, not whispering but not really wanting anyone else to hear either, "was that him?"

"Hmm," I said as I puffed on the pipe, pretending

to be interested in all the news that he was catching me up on.

"But that wasn't his house?"

"No."

"So, I am right in assuming that was not his wife, either?"

"Certainly not."

"Naughty man."

"Quite," I muttered, the pipe bouncing around in my mouth as I did so. Christopher continued to pretend to regale me with stories about his young niece and nephew and how well they were doing at school, annoyingly loudly as two elderly women passed by on the other side of the street. They did not take too much notice of us, and I was quite sure that they wouldn't have been able to hear a single thing, they were that old, but Christopher was keen to keep up the charade to the very best of his ability.

"I wonder what he's doing in there," he said wistfully looking up the street towards the door that he had disappeared behind.

"I can take a pretty good guess," I muttered, as I checked over Christopher's shoulder to make sure there was no one behind. "Am I clear behind me?"

"Yes, why?"

I lifted the front of my shirt up and pulled out the small, well-concealed pistol that had been rubbing against my bladder for the last hour or so. Slowly, I pulled it out, taking a firm grasp of the grip, fearful that I would for some reason end up dropping the article.

Even slower than before, I pulled the top slide back until I heard a slight click, then looked down to make sure I could see a small round waiting in the chamber. I let the slide back forward with a clunk, a little louder than I had anticipated.

"What are you doing?" Christopher said, panicked, his eyes wide and carelessly looking down towards the weapon.

"What do you think? Keep your head up, will you?"

He did as he was told and I noticed that the perspiration was already running down his head, his spectacles sliding forward on his nose, forcing him to push them back into place.

"No. It's not right. There must be a better way."

"What do you mean?" I growled, as I withdrew the pipe from my mouth and put a finger over the bowl in an attempt to extinguish it. "This is the perfect way. We've just caught the old goat sneaking into some other woman's house that isn't his own. If we can confront him here, then we can save a lot of time and effort which, if you recall, we don't have a lot of."

He looked as if he was going to cry, but still somehow managed to remain calm and composed and, if someone was to walk past us, they would have had no idea that we were in the middle of a mild disagreement.

"No, there is another way. There is always another way. If you try and blackmail him into some sort of agreement, then he will be more inclined to want to push back against you later on. If we can save him some sort of embarrassment now, then he might be far more helpful in the long run. That is what this is all about isn't it?" he gesticulated, encompassing the entire street.

"Scoring points against the Germans in the long run. We could score a goal against them now, or we could score a hattrick against them over the next couple of months."

"What do you propose then?" I growled, frustratingly putting the pistol back down my trousers, carefully so that it didn't fall down one of my trouser legs.

He thought things through for a moment, the perspiration subsiding as he realised that he was winning the battle, for now. Instead, beads of sweat began to form on my own hands, as I realised that we were now two men, standing in the middle of a street, not saying anything to one another. We were beginning to stick out.

"We will make our way to his home. Then we will simply have to wait for him to return."

"Alright. There is a phone box a few streets away. I will call Jules and tell him to get the other two to come with us to confront him."

"No, not confront. Talk to him."

"Alright then, talk to him," I was growing frustrated with him and needed desperately to get away from the street and feel like I was getting some fresher air. In the loudest French that I deemed appropriate, I announced that Christopher must join me for a cup of coffee, to continue our catch up, before we made good our escape without looking back.

I felt Christopher relax as we padded away from the house, still clearly worried that I had even considered entering the building with a weapon drawn, but nonetheless encouraged that he had managed to talk me round. He became so relaxed that he even started talking, which did nothing but make me more uptight.

I grew uncomfortable with his questions, as he asked about my family, to the point where I knew I had to redirect the conversation.

"And, Christophe, what about you? What is your background?"

He didn't seem as uncomfortable about the probing question as I had thought he would have been, especially given the nature of his beliefs, but all in all, he appeared, for the first time, quite open. Almost normal.

"My father, he fought in the first war. Was gassed at *Ypres*. He was never the same. All I can remember of my childhood was the coughing, sometimes mucus, often blood. Anyway, he died when I was twelve or so. And I vowed to never become involved in fighting a war for as long as I lived.

"Then this old thing kicked off. At first, I stuck to my guns, if you'll pardon the expression, became a firefighter. All those bombs. Worse than what we had seen the other day."

For the first time since he started speaking, he broke off, turning away from me and I could clearly see that he was dabbing away at some tears. When he turned to the front again, I could see that he was no longer with me, he was somewhere else, somewhere far more harrowing.

"I've seen houses collapse around men as they stepped into them. Fires engulfing entire streets. I've seen things that you would never believe."

I hesitated for a moment as he took in a large gulp of air.

"Oh, I believe them alright. I have seen my fair share of what German bombs can do to a person."

He looked at me and almost instantly understood. It was the first time that I had any kind of feeling that could have been mistaken for affection for the man.

13

I had never seen so many knees bouncing around in anticipation as I had done while I sat in Raymond Peintre's living room. The chair that I was in was incredibly comfortable, but every bone in my body seemed as if it was out of place and disjointed, as I realised that until I was out of the house, out of the situation, I would not be able to relax.

Everything that I could think of to distract myself and simply cope with the situation had been employed, and failed, from counting the number of glasses that I could see displayed, to simply closing my eyes and embracing the darkness.

Instead, I had to settle for watching everyone else, and how their nerves manifested. There was a slight comfort in the fact that I was not alone, and that the people that I was with knew exactly what was expected from them and their role in the matter. But there was still the eternal fear that it would be me who messed up, it would be me who failed in their duty.

So far though, everything had gone swimmingly. Madame Peintre had been only too happy to allow these four friends of her husband into her home, to talk to him about his work in a most urgent manner. The poor lady had no idea that she had just invited four potential killers into her home, who would likely end up threatening her husband to get their way. If she did have an idea, then I doubted very much that we would have been offered as much coffee and sandwiches as she had done.

As Madame Peintre left the room again, I began to think of her husband, and his funny little walk that he possessed as I had followed him around. It was odd that I had seen more of the man's back than I had his front and wondered what his face would look like once I had been able to survey it.

I could still recall the very first time that I had seen Raymond Peintre's name, on a crate in the station yard that we had been in to switch labels over. I had no idea at the time that Raymond had been the sole owner of the factory before the war, but now demoted to foreman as German replacements were sourced to oversee the production of engine parts.

Our presence in his house, and what we were about to attempt, was going to be a big risk, but one that we had deemed necessary for success. There was a large chance that he was in regular contact with the Germans about the various goings-on inside the factory, and that all he would have to do would be to mention it to his supervisor the next time he went to work.

It was an eventuality that seemed all the more likely to me once I had seen the house that he was living in. It was virtually palatial, and I could not help but wonder how a man, even one who owned an entire factory, would be able to afford the place that he called home.

I had never seen such vibrant and exquisite colours hanging from windows until I found myself enthralled by the Peintre's curtains, some window panes quite clearly brand new. I questioned what kind of a man that we were confronting that was able to replace the glass in his windows as quickly as they were blasted out.

The door to the living room was shut tight, but we were still able to hear the crunch of the front door as it was opened and closed, and the shuffle of Peintre's wife as she scurried past the door to greet her husband.

We all looked at one another, preparing ourselves for what was about to happen. The plan that we had was in place, but I could only wonder at how far awry it was going to go. All manner of things might happen, up to and including an arrest party bounding through the door. If that was the case, then I knew it would have been my fault; Christopher and I had stood in that street for too long. We had aroused suspicion.

There was a muttering out in the hallway, as a man's voice, strained and concerned, gruffly berated his wife for simply letting the men in. They could have been anyone after all. She ought to have been more careful.

She promised never to do such a thing again and shuffled back down the hallway.

I almost felt the big exhale of breath as Raymond Peintre placed his hand on the door handle and turned, as everyone on the other side of the door did exactly the same thing.

The first thing I noticed about the man was that he had a face that I had not been expecting. I did not know why, but his posture and stature was one that told me that he had been in possession of an old, wearisome face, one that should have been weathered and battered.

But, in actual fact, he seemed quite young, his skin pale and soft and, had it not been for the great bushy beard that dangled from his chin, he would have perhaps looked younger still.

His eyes grew wide at the sight of the men in his house, but he was not overly concerned. It was almost as if he had come to expect this sort of thing.

The only hint of fear that I could glean from his expression was when Mike glided in behind him, closing the door and shutting off his exit. Even I had to admit that the fear would close in then. No man likes to have his only exit point cut off.

"Raymond Peintre?" I asked confidently, standing

from the chair and placing my hands behind my back, as if I was a barrister.

He said nothing, but stared back at me defiantly, his frame far smaller than mine but as he puffed his chest out, he seemed to grow to the point where he had the upper hand.

"My name is Jean Pelletier. We are here to talk to you about your factory."

Still, he refused to speak, but silently manoeuvred around the room until he found a spot to sit. He withdrew a packet of cigarettes and lit one, before finally acknowledging that I was in the room by motioning me to continue.

"The Allies have been bombing around the local area for a considerable amount of time, causing a great amount of devastation and loss of life. This has happened without much of the factory being hit and with negligible effects on the production of engine parts for the German war machine."

He continued to stare at me, with no significant look on his face, apart from one of slight annoyance that he was already aware of the situation that had befallen his local area.

"In short, Monsieur Peintre, we would like your help in stopping the German ability to use your factory, without the need for significant bombing raids from the RAF."

I could sense the growing frustration around the room, even Christopher, a recently converted pacifist was shuffling around, his knuckles tightening as I saw him lining up a decent punch to the man's nose.

Despite the obvious tension, Raymond Peintre seemed intent on finishing his first cigarette, all the while keeping a firm stare with me, before he made any kind of noise. Once finished, he stubbed it out in a tray to his left, before withdrawing the packet again and lighting a second cigarette.

Just as I thought that we were going to have to wait for him to smoke his way through an entire packet before we made any progress, he spoke. His voice was inevitably rough and gravelly, the result of years of chain-smoking his way through any stressful situation, but what he said was neither an offence to my ears or music to them.

"I want the Germans out of my country as much as the next Frenchman. I despise them for what they have taken from me, and my family, but I don't know you. You could be anyone. So no, I won't help you, unless you can prove who you are."

There was a swift movement from somewhere in my peripheral vision, and I was not too surprised to see that it had been Mike that had snapped first.

His pistol was drawn and soon pressing into the temple on Peintre's head, the veins popping out to the surface of his skin as Mike pressed deeper into it.

"Does this prove who we are for you? Would the Germans do this to you if it was some sort of trap?"

Peintre remained calm, and even had the audacity to bring the cigarette to his lips for a drag.

"Yes. Of course, they would. Only they wouldn't lose control like that. They would have done it far more calmly."

Christopher got up from his chair and gently pulled at Mike's shoulders, lowering the pistol as he did so. Mike got the message and tucked the pistol away again, taking a leaf out of Peintre's book and lighting up a cigarette to calm himself down. Before too long it was difficult to see what was going on, there seemed to be that much smoke in the room.

Christopher smiled sympathetically at the man, before taking a chair opposite him and introducing himself.

"I'm Christophe Hanot. Excuse my friends, they are tired of the war."

"We all are," Peintre said, to which Christopher scoffed, not in a mocking way, but an understanding one.

"Look, my friend," he said, looking up to see if he had got any kind of negative reaction, "we need your help. Too many people are dying around here. And it is because of your factory. If we were able to verify who we claim to be, then would you consider helping us?"

He looked around nervously, stubbing his cigarette out with one final flourish.

"Are you from Britain?"

"What makes you say that?"

"No Frenchman that I know would be so heavy-handed in their approach to a matter such as this."

Christophe smirked and shrugged, conceding that his compatriots had not gone about things in the best way.

"Then yes, we were sent by London."

He still did not seem convinced. As he thought about whether he should light another cigarette, Christopher was growing impatient.

"Do you listen to *Radio Londres?*"

"Of course, everyone does. I daresay even the Germans do."

"Then give us a message. We can get it transmitted for you. Then you will know that we are who we say we are. Not just some phoneys."

As Christopher spoke, there was a knock on the front door. Everyone turned to each other in panic, convinced that one side had set the other up. Peintre looked to me as if to question whether I had any other friends preparing to drop by, while we all glared at him as if he had somehow set us up.

With horror billowing from all of our eyes, we heard the dutiful Madame Peintre slide towards the door, before greeting whoever it was that was there. We all prayed that she heeded the advice of her husband but either the visitor was persistent, or Peintre's wife had a shorter memory than a goldfish.

As the figure walked into the room, I felt sick to my stomach as I saw his face. In actuality, there were worse persons that could have joined us at that moment in time but Philippe, one of the local police officers, was not a face that I particularly enjoyed seeing.

It took him a moment or two to realise who we were, which was understandable as we had normally seen him when covered in a thick coating of brick dust the night after a heavy air raid.

"You?" he mumbled, before taking a slight step backwards. It was futile, the same plan had been put into action the second that he walked through the door; Mike was already blocking his only exit.

There was a brief moment of panic on everyone's face, as we wondered what was going to happen next but, fortunately, Mike did not seem so determined to draw his pistol again.

"What's going on here?"

"*Salut,* Philippe," Peintre said, rising from his chair and taking the officer's hand. "Please, sit."

The police officer obliged, knowing that he did not really have too many other options at his disposal. But it seemed to diffuse the situation somewhat.

"Don't worry," Peintre said, looking at us in turn. "Philippe is a friend. A trustworthy one. Especially after I see to it that his family will have a good Christmas."

He chuckled, a hearty one, before belching and coughing his way through to another cigarette.

"Any message that I choose?" he asked, looking back to Christopher for the first time since the police officer had entered the room.

There was still panic drilled into Christopher's

face, which was understandable, as we had no idea if we could trust either of the men in the room. But we had little choice. We were in over our heads and, if they did turn out to be German informants, we would know soon enough.

"Anything you want Raymond."

14

I had never felt quite so nervous in all my life. There was a plethora of things for me to worry over, and each one of them was taking its place in the carousel of my mind, as the rate of my heart grew more rapid and the viscosity of my blood thickened.

In my short life, more so in the years that I had been to war, I realised that there were two types of fear. There was the fear that drove men on, gave them an overwhelming, yet elusive confidence to press on, to do the very thing that it would take to escape the situation that one was in. The other fear was a crippling one, that made men sit in a corner of a room, catatonic, staring at nothing in particular and thinking only of how hopeless their situation truly was.

It was the second, paralytic fear, that was gripping me.

The apprehension was unbelievable, the likes of which I had never experienced before, not even when racing to the cockpit of my Hurricane, knowing that I could have been running to my own plywood coffin.

I tried to draw the distinguishing features of that fear, the type that had still allowed me to function, and to focus on it, pulling myself back from the brink. But I could find nothing.

That life seemed so far away now, the long drawn-out summer evenings in the local pub, raising a glass to another poor fellow who had got himself shot down or hours of sitting in deck chairs reading, waiting for the *Luftwaffe* to give us something to do.

At times it had seemed like an almost idyllic existence until the bell rung, and men began to disperse all over the field, a blind patriotism driving them to their own demise.

The carousel turned again though, as I lost sight of those summer scrambles and came face to face with the figure of the police officer, Philippe, who now threatened our entire existence.

There was nothing that we could have done. We couldn't have interrupted Peintre as he tried to negotiate a settlement but, equally, we couldn't have disposed of the poor man simply for wanting to visit a friend. But it was that element of not being in control, the very fact that our survival now depended on a factory foreman and policeman, that was causing my heart to flutter in the manner that it was.

I could not help myself but keep thinking of the training that we had gone through, the way in which that we were supposed to get alongside them, befriend them, before attempting to pay them off. We were taught to make friends with our subjects, as it is far harder to betray a friend, than it is an acquaintance, especially when our enemy could throw far more money at them than we ever could.

Bribery was an art, one that took time to nurture and develop and one, if carried out properly, that could lead to very big rewards indeed.

But our approach to Philippe had been nothing short of a butchery, a scene that, had our directing staff at Arisaig known would happen, we would never have made it past our mysterious interviews.

I cringed at the mobhanded and unrefined way that Peintre had offered his friend the chance to make some extra cash, and refrained from burying my head in my hands like I had done as we had sat in the man's house.

But I had to keep reminding myself, as the carousel gaily turned, we had been left with little choice. In fact, the relief that I had experienced, upon hearing that the two men were good friends, had been overwhelming. That friendship had given us all a second chance. We knew that there wouldn't be a third.

My mind soon began to wander, away from the police officer, and to the man who had made him the offer.

Once upon a time, when I had been at university, I had known some people who would have described Raymond Peintre as a dirty capitalist, someone who only cared for himself and how deep his pockets became.

And, from what I had seen of his home, elements of that had been true. The glass in his windows were swiftly replaced, while that of his struggling neighbourhood would remain glassless for a long time.

His home spoke of a tale of frustration, one that plainly laid bare the fall from grace of heir to a large automobile empire, to humble foreman. There was money everywhere that I had looked and I daresay that he had a franc or two tucked under the mattress of his bed.

"Do you think we can trust him?" Mike asked, not for the first time.

"Who are you talking about now?"

"The factory owner. What's to stop him from going and having a chinwag with the Germans? They might pay him a bit more."

"Same goes for the policeman."

"True," he muttered, sighing as he heaved himself up from his chair. "Drink?"

I shook my head, as he gently nudged Christopher's foot to ask him the same question. He recoiled aggressively, as if the touch had reminded him of some ghastly experience as a child.

His face was flushed, and a thin film of sweat had been pulled right the way over his face. His unathletic and stocky body was curled up into a tight ball, something that looked almost impossible for him.

It wasn't difficult to see, that Christopher was

thinking far too heavily about things, but Mike decided that it was a good time to push him to the edge. I knew why he did it, I had known him for a long time after all. He had done so with many of the other boys that we had known whilst studying, but often Mike's way of geeing somebody up and coaxing them from a trance, had the innate ability to simply infuriate and frustrate.

"What's up with you?" he said, trying again to knock at Christopher's legs to induce the same reaction. "I only asked if you wanted a drink."

"I don't want one of your rotten drinks!" Christopher exploded, his legs shooting out as if the jack in the box had been wound up months ago, ready to spring up ferociously.

Mike's lips pursed, as he poised himself for a good fight, sharpening his tongue in preparation for some witty, but spiteful comeback.

But, to my surprise, nothing of the sort materialised. Instead, quite the opposite occurred.

"Sorry, Christopher. Sorry."

I almost stood to attention in the middle of the room and demanded to know what was happening. The world seemed quite as if it had been turned on its head. Christopher was showing elements of aggression that I did not know he possessed, while Mike displayed components of something resembling self-restraint. Judging by the look on Mike's face, even he was not aware that he was capable of such a virtue.

My mouth rather inadvertently hung open as he

traipsed around the room, my eyes glaring at him, wanting to catch his eye so that I could burst out laughing. But the sincerity etched into his stare told me that something deeper had occurred, a change in his manner that had more far-reaching effects than I could have guessed at.

It was at that moment that I realised that his whole demeanour was slowly changing. Bar the odd outburst and moment of aggression, his mind seemed transformed. Gone was the blood lust that would have seen him kill anyone who even knew a single German word and there was the rational, compassionate side of his mind.

Gone too was the sharp tongue, as pointed as a dagger, that had done far more damage than a steel blade ever could have done, marking the arrival of something that was the infancy of consideration.

He seemed more thoughtful, able to lose himself in the company of his own mind, something that he had never been able to do before, in all the time that I had known him. He had frequently got bored of himself, always looking to join with others for his entertainment.

But, forlorn, he now sat, sipping away at his drink staring into the hearth of the fireplace. I did not know it for sure, but I guessed at what he was thinking of, or rather *who*.

I had never seen the girl that he had claimed to have fallen in love with, not until we had the *Gestapo* on our tails and needed a way out of *Tours.* She was a pretty young girl, maybe edging on a stereotype of what I might have expected of Mike, but pleasant nonetheless and, just as in love with Mike as he was with her. To the point that she willing to help us escape.

I could not help myself but think of Suzanne, who had loved her own country in much the same way that Mike had loved his girl. She had sacrificed her husband in its darkest hour, been blown up a handful of times and then been prepared to step in front of a bullet.

The sharp pang of my heart told me how much I truly missed her, not just the grounding that she gave me, a rationality, but the moments that we had shared nothing but silence. We had been content in the presence of one another and, on occasion, the physical contact that still had the effect of making my arm hairs stand to attention.

Despite all that, I did not think that I loved her, not in the common sense of the word. We had shared something, something that no one else around us could quite comprehend. It was the loss that we had experienced, the complete feeling of utter despair at the realisation that the people who mean the most to you will never know of your presence ever again.

For her, it had been her husband, a pilot killed in the early months of the war. For me, it was my dear wife and son, the very thought of whom threatened tears to begin streaming down my cheeks.

But there seemed enough fragility and vulnerability in the room, and I decided against letting the horrors of my own memories get the better of me.

Instead, I engaged my imagination, trying to picture what it would have been like the moment that Suzanne had crossed the border, to be greeted by her father in law, Alfred. He too had been a great source of comfort to me, and I had been mightily relieved to find out that he was not actually dead, but very much alive.

The thought of the two of them enjoying Switzerland seemed so distant, the chasm widening at the realisation that Suzanne may never have made it that far.

"Jean!" came the cry that I had been waiting for all evening.

"Georges! How are you, my young friend?"

"Papa says that you are all very tired. But all I see you do is sitting here and listening to the wireless. How can you be tired?"

I chuckled softly, as the tears over a lost bond with my own son began to get the better of me.

"I suppose that it is our old bodies, little one. I could only wish that we could have as busy a life as yours and still have so much energy."

"Hush, hush," Andrew rasped, his palm flapping up and down as he did so. Everyone knew what it meant, including the young Georges. It was time for the important bit on *Radio Londres.*

Dot dot dot dah.

It was a drum beat that I had long learnt to

revere, as it thumped out the Morse for 'V,' and each time it belted out it felt like an even bigger victory than the letter it represented.

Then came Georges' favourite part, the waves and twinkles of foreign notes in the background, as the Germans tried desperately to disrupt the signal from reaching the homes of the people they subjugated.

A weird jumble of rather odd poetry began to be read out, and I could only dream of what each line would mean to the men and women that were, as we were, crouched around a small wireless set and listening desperately for something that we recognised.

I looked at Mike, who seemed like he was alive with schoolboy mischief and rascality once again.

I just hope that Peintre is listening as hard as we are.

Then, after a few minutes, there were a few words that I could recognise.

"*Nathalie, tes tomates sont mûres.*"

And that was that.

"Was that it?" Andrew asked, speaking over the announcer mid-flow.

"Shut up! Shush!" Christopher called out to us, edging so far forward on his chair that he was about to fall off.

We waited for a few moments more, listening in to messages that would have little meaning and almost no consequence for us. But still, at Christopher's insistence, and due to his volatility, we obliged.

"Yes, that was it," I replied, my throat hoarse from

the tension that was hardening every sinew in my body.

"Nathalie, your tomatoes are ripe. I wonder who Nathalie is?" Mike mused aloud, to no one in particular. "Why Nathalie?"

"His daughter? His wife?" I suggested. "We'll never know, Mike."

"Well, I know," Jules said, propping himself up in the doorway. "And it most definitely isn't his daughter. Nor his wife."

"Sly old dog," Mike said, smiling a big, broad grin, proud of the old mischief-maker.

15

Raymond Peintre had seemed to age significantly in the short time since we had visited him last, the great frown lines having deepened somehow and the laughter lines around his mouth fading until they were almost invisible.

There was a sincerity about him now that he had previously not possessed, although I could not quite put my finger on what it was that made me think so. Perhaps it was because my fuse had started to shorten, the looming deadline which would clang with the sound of bombs whistling down on this part of France.

Mike and I were free to leave whenever we felt like we were in danger, but I could not see how we could ever part with the town of *Besançon.* There was something about it that had captured our hearts, despite the fact we had nothing for us to call our own. Maybe it was the feeling that we were actually making a tangible difference, to the town, but also on the wider war. If we could pull this off the Germans would not be churning out as many engine parts as they could have done. Without those engines, they couldn't make tanks, planes, staff cars, the list was as long as my arm.

But it was equally as likely to be the feeling of a home that we had received in the warmth of Jules' house. He had welcomed us with arms wide and helped us to truly feel like part of his family. Georges was a constant morale booster for us all, the war not able to fully corrupt his innocent little mind.

We had nothing to fear, according to him, nothing to be sad about. He was partly right. We had nothing to be sad about, as long as we accepted that we would be dead before the end of the war, and that was the one thing that I feared the most.

The fact that the way I would perish would be at the hand of my own nation's bombs only served to exacerbate that fear.

"Raymond," I said, as he interrupted me with the palm of his hand. I stopped abruptly as I saw the cogs begin to whir in the back of his mind, his eyes sinking into their sockets as he withdrew from the world that we were in.

His lips curled and twitched as if he was possessed by some evil spirit, but the cynic told me that all he was attempting to do was to work out how he could earn himself a little bit more money.

"This way," he said eventually, his head jerking like his mind was still in the clutches of some demonic being. He led us through hallways of great grandeur and opulence, before taking us upstairs to carry on the tour of magnificent paintings and exquisite artefacts.

"It's like the British museum," Mike muttered under his breath. I had to agree with him. The walls were filled with shelves of objects that appeared as if they had been taken from a colonial conquest, from more countries than I could ever name.

"In here," he said with an outstretched arm. "It will be safer."

Mike grinned at him as he pushed past him and into the room, "Don't trust your wife, Peintre? Wise move, wise move. My father always told me much the same about women."

Peintre glared at him with a stare so cold that I thought Mike might freeze on the spot. Panicking, and just a little short of breath, Mike sensed that he may have made an error of judgement.

"A lovely house, Monsieur Peintre. Beautiful. Quite a wonder that the Germans haven't taken it for one of their own."

Peintre lifted his plump, oval-shaped head, in an attempt to look down his nose ever so slightly at us. He wanted the two men before him to know who was in control here, even if we didn't believe it.

"And why would they do that?" his question was asked with gravitas and confidence, almost making me believe that he was genuinely confused at such a proposition.

The more that I dealt with him, the more that I realised that Peintre would have made an excellent politician. From what I had seen of him so far, I had seen him able to deceive his wife excellently, while also manipulating his voice to such a degree that I almost believed he was none the wiser about Mike's suggestion.

It was possibly what had made him all the money in the first place.

"Monsieur Peintre, did you listen to *Radio Londres* yesterday evening?"

He turned away from us and staggered towards the window, as if he was in great pain. Mike looked at me and, tapping his watch, started to make gestures that he thought the man had knocked back a drink or two. It was possible.

He hadn't been involved in this war like we had, and to then have something like this thrust upon his shoulders could not have been easy for him.

Or maybe his wife had found out about the girl that we had seen him with the day before.

He stroked his beard like some wise old guru, as he stared at, rather than out, the window and sighed. I had tried to guess at what it was that was distracting him, but nothing that I could come up with seemed to justify how one man could be so inattentive as he was.

He half-turned, turning to the large oak desk that

was standing faithfully to his left, and he started to twist and turn discarded pieces of paper, that looked as though they had been dumped there months ago. Maybe they were props, to impress people who stepped into his study, or perhaps they had been the last bits of paperwork that he had to deal with before the Germans had commandeered his facility.

Whatever it was, it was making his face morph from one of sincerity to utter depression.

"Yes. I listened to it," he mumbled, losing all sense of authority as he sank into a leather chair, rubbing at his equally leathery skin.

He said nothing further, frustrating us both no end as he refused to elaborate on what he had heard.

Each time that Mike or I stepped forward to say something, he drew a deep breath in, quite like he was about to let out a great bellow or cry. Every time that he did, we recoiled, keen to allow him to speak in his own time.

But time was not something that we had in abundance. We had already used four days of our limited allocation and we had barely even had a chance to look at the perimeter of the factory yet. We desperately needed a decision from the man in front of us, and fast.

"So?" Mike said, clearing his throat with a slight wobble. "Can you help us?"

"*Will* you help us?" I repeated after yet another silence. If it wasn't for the faint muttering under his breath as he thought aloud, we would have both been forgiven for thinking that the man had suddenly been struck dumb.

There was something odd about the air in that room, as it made me feel queasy and uptight, a great weight pressing down on my chest the longer that I stayed in there. It also made me feel incredibly suspicious of everyone; Peintre, Philippe the police officer, even Mike and myself were called into question a couple of times.

But the biggest worry lay with Peintre. It almost felt like he was biding his time, waiting for something to happen.

My knee began to quiver slightly as my body started to panic. I was still in full control of my mind and rationality, but I was aware that if I allowed the situation to carry on unchecked, then that would soon be on its way out also.

"Monsieur Peintre, please. Will you help us? We do not have much time. The bombers will only stay away for so long. They want your factory destroyed. We have only been given a small window in which to operate."

"What do you want me to do?!" he suddenly blurted, his hands thrown to the sky in exasperation. His cheeks had reddened nicely, similar to how I imagined Nathalie's tomatoes were looking now they were ready for picking. "You are going to carry on with your plan whether I am with you or not, aren't you?"

It was the first time since I had met him that I felt sorry for him. I hadn't taken to him much, he had a lovely home and a pleasant enough wife, and he was willing to squander it all on some little girl that cared for nothing but his money.

But, in that outburst, I had realised that he was genuinely worried, scared even, about what was going to happen. This was unfamiliar territory for him, and it was clear to see that he was not happy about it, but the two men in his home would not leave until they had got their answer.

I tried to be as soft as I could, channelling everything that I had learnt from Christopher and trying to invoke a similar response.

"Raymond, we need your blessing for this to happen. You know the factory, you're in the best place possible to help. Without you, there will be a great deal more lives that will be lost."

"With your help, we can do maximum damage to small parts of the factory. From the outside, it won't have changed in the slightest. The same can't be said if the bombers come back."

He looked me straight in the eyes, and something told me that I had to tell him what we had planned.

"We know that the Germans rely heavily on your equipment; your presses, your lathes, the boring equipment. Without that, they won't be able to produce enough engines. That will stop their advances in other regions and help the Allies when they return," he scoffed, and Mike did well to not let his frustrations bubble over.

"We want to enter your factory and identify the machines that are crucial to the Germans. Then, we'll plant explosives on them and destroy them for a long period of time. The British government will reimburse you after the war."

He lit a cigarette, that bounced around excitably as he began to grow irate, wagging his finger at us like naughty children.

"Let me tell you something. My grandfather built that factory. It was nothing more than a garden shed when he started, he drove himself to an early grave, as did my father, making sure that it carried on going. We found success, and that success we shared with the people here, without that factory they would not have jobs. They would barely have lives to live.

"And now? Now you want me to help you blow all that up. You want me to destroy my own factory?"

He let the question linger in the air for a second or two, as he took in such a large drag of his cigarette that it was almost reduced to the stub.

"I have my own ways of resistance. I am not as idle as you and your government think I am. Clutches. We can make hundreds of them a week. Most of them work to perfection, but I make sure that one or two are faulty. They won't see out fifty kilometres. That takes time for them to resolve, men, resources. Are you saying I am not doing enough?"

He had gone into full businessman mode, there

was nothing to do other than take a firm grasp of the situation, shocking him into submission.

"No, you are not. Most of your manufactures work, and that is what is killing innocent people. If you help us, *nothing* will come out of that factory of *any* use to the Germans."

I felt Mike suck in air through his gritted teeth as he thought that I had taken it too far, his hand almost reaching over to my arm to hold me back, but I was in full flow.

"Thirty-two people died in a single bombing raid the night before last. Fifty in the three raids before that. All of those bombs were meant to land on the factory, crippling it for weeks. How long did it remain closed for? Three hours. Three hours. Just one bomb made it inside the perimeter fence, and the backup generator was working to full capacity by sunrise. You may think that you are doing your bit, Raymond, but the fact is you could be doing more."

I finished my speech and felt like collapsing into the nearest chair that I could find, it was the closest thing to an inspirational speech that I could muster, and it had sapped all of my energy.

I watched his face, trying to read any signs that would give him away, but there was next to nothing. He chewed on the end of his cigarette, the soggy saliva that rolled around on his lips glistening in the late morning sun.

Suddenly, he shot to his feet, straight-backed and energetic once more. The distant look in his eyes had vanished, as if reinvigorated and convinced by the enthusiastic man before him.

I turned to Mike and gave a flick of my eyebrows. He shook his head as he looked away, smirking.

He pulled something taped to the underside of his desk and turned to face us. In his hand he had a large wallet, from which he pulled some papers and spread them out in front of us.

"Plans. For the factory. They lay out everything that is in there."

"How recent are they?" Mike asked.

"I had them made the week before the Germans occupied *Besançon.* Don't worry," he said looking at our concerned faces, "they haven't done anything to change the inside. But you'll have to figure out where the sentries are yourself.

"I will give you a name," he said, stepping away from the plans and offering us both a cigarette. "He will help you. Knows the factory better than I do."

He lit our cigarettes with a slight tremble in his hand, which I hoped was excitement.

"After that, I want nothing to do with what goes on. I don't want to see you again. The Germans are going to suspect that I had something to do with it from the start. Let me at least try and keep my family safe by keeping my hands clean."

Mike and I silently nodded, before folding the plans up and tucking them away for no one else to see.

Peintre said nothing to us as we bundled together

what information he had given to us and made for the front door. It was only as we went to leave that he held out his hand to us and whispered those two words that every saboteur loved to hear.

"*Bon chance.*"

16

It was incredibly difficult, having studied the floor-plans of the factory for so long, to tear my eyes away from its gated perimeter. But break my gaze I must as I was aware that any one of the other occupants of the café might have been a German agent, ready to use my longing glares as evidence against me.

My coffee had gone cold a long time ago, and the conversation between Jules and me had gone the same way. Instead, we sat and smoked, occasionally grunting something to each other as the minutes slowly ticked by.

Jules was calm, relaxed, as he perused the newspaper with gusto, the ink rubbing off slightly on the tips of his fingers.

I, on the other hand, could not distract myself totally from the disproportionate number of soldiers compared to the local population. It seemed that, especially so in the café, that there were three

German soldiers for every Frenchman, to the point where German was the predominant language that I had heard as we wandered towards the café.

The rest of the customers were dressed in faded blue overalls, every other body tying the top half of the boiler suit around his waist, revealing the greasy and dirtied arms and hands that could only have come about as a result of hours on a workshop floor.

I lit another cigarette, allowing myself another brief look towards the gates of the factory. Two guards took their posts as they continued to pace up and down, basking in the warmth of the sunshine on an otherwise quite nippy afternoon.

"Stop it," Jules growled as he turned another page to pretend to read.

"Stop what?"

He didn't answer, instead flicking backwards and forwards in *Au Pilori*, the weekly newspaper that the Germans were only too happy to distribute to the French people. He caught my eye, as I took in the cartoon on the front page of the paper, a sketched image of three men in stocks; a Priest, a Rabbi and a traveller.

Menteur, Voleur, Assassin was scribbled under each caricature.

Liar, thief, murderer.

Jules raised an eyebrow at me, informing me that he took it all with as much disgust as I had written across my face, which I was glad about, especially after reading the headline at the top of the page.

Les Anglais abandonneront!

The English will give up.

“Ignore it. They say plenty about the Jews that isn’t true either.”

I grunted at him, as he folded it up and tucked it underneath his crossed arms.

“So, you haven’t said, did it all go alright last night?”

His eyebrows dropped back down to their natural height, although one was slightly higher than the other as his curiosity got the better of him.

“What?” I blurted, my mind’s instant reaction as it bought itself some time to work out what it was that I was going to say.

I knew immediately what he had meant, but it had nonetheless shocked me into regurgitating the events of the night previous, where we collected the items that we had requested from London.

Mike had an annoying habit of referring to it as our ‘shopping,’ which was why I was quite glad that I was with Jules, so as not to hear him call it that again.

Mike had changed over the last month or two, his lust for blood had waned dramatically, but the carefree way that he was referring to the explosives and weapons that could potentially kill many lives frustrated me no end.

“Fine,” I said curtly. “It went fine. We got what we needed.”

I tried my best to swallow the repeated feeling of claustrophobia, the paranoid sense that someone had always been watching us and tracking our every move. It had become even more strong after receiving the news about our local SS officer, Captain Murky as he had become labelled.

I had tried to do my best to dig into the myths about him from earlier on in the war, to find out if there was any truth in the allegations that he had killed numerous unarmed, surrendering soldiers when the Germans had first invaded. But nothing I found was definitive. In many ways, I was glad that was the case.

Nevertheless, the rumours were enough for me, and I had spent the night retrieving the canisters packed with bombs and guns, convinced that within the next ten seconds that trap would be sprung upon us.

But it never came.

The weapons were now carefully stored in an underground storage shed, built by a local farmer in the hope that, if the Germans were to search his premises, they would be drawn to the most obvious, but best hiding place; his barn.

"Good. Good," Jules mumbled, his wry smile and glinting eyes making plain his accusation that I was lying to him. I wondered if my own eyes were managing to hide the guilt as well as I was hoping.

"Are you sure you will recognise him?" I asked, trying to draw away some of the heat from my flushing face. "The contact that Peintre has given us. Will you be absolutely certain it is him?"

His face dropped, not in a despondent way, but one that was more relaxed in its nature.

"Of course," he said, without smiling, "I grew up with him. I know his whole family. Fat little face, with cheeks as red as apples, but an athletic frame. Tall, wiry, hair as white as snow. I will always remember the back of his head most as I chased him during our school races."

"Let's hope he walks in backwards then," I mumbled, mistakenly taking a sip of the icy cold coffee. Forcing it down to avoid drawing attention to myself, Jules laughed to himself quietly.

I pulled my wristwatch up to my eyeline and checked.

"How long now?"

"Three minutes."

"Why twelve thirty-seven? Why not twelve-thirty or forty?"

I could not be bothered to go into the ins and outs of what my training had involved, in order to get to the bottom of his question. But I rapidly found myself back in Arisaig, listening to the strong arguments for setting odd times for meetings. It was to make it more difficult for the Germans to follow us, or spot suspicious activity.

Locals met each other at odd times all through the day, but agents always kept religiously to their timetables. It was easy to remember a meeting at eleven o'clock, or one-thirty in the afternoon, but less so for twelve thirty-seven.

It was hoped that it would add a layer of fog to any observations that were on us, while simultaneously adding a façade of legitimacy.

I watched impatiently as the second hand rolled around my watch face, my palms growing sweatier by the second. If the man was late, even by something as marginal as ten seconds, he would turn up to the café with no one to meet.

A meeting that was not kept to was a meeting that would easily be compromised.

The claustrophobia that I had experienced so often in the past was reaching a climax, one that did not go through a fleeting stage but was lasting hours at best, days more often than not.

It was a restrictive crushing of my chest that got to me first and, as my breathing grew shallower and more rapid, so too did my heart rate. It was a slippery slope that would almost always lead to nausea and dizziness. It wasn't the finest attribute for someone who was required to come into contact with his enemy on a daily basis.

"Thirty-seven is my lucky number," I replied, leaving far too long a gap to answer my accomplice.

I took a slither of comfort from the fact that I did not feel like I was sticking out too much, which was what I always felt like whenever I went anywhere with Mike. Not only was Jules a local, but he had that kind of face that no one really took too much notice of, the perfect face to become a criminal on the run.

Might come in handy soon.

But his common and run-of-the-mill face was exactly what I wanted in that moment, as I could not risk having too many unfamiliar faces around the café. Besides, three men sharing a coffee was far more inconspicuous than a group of six or seven doing the same thing.

I jumped as the sound of the outside world intensified as the café door was opened, and just as quickly slammed shut again. A blast of cold air slapped me in the face, and I could feel the icy glare of Jules as he wondered what it was that he had let himself in for.

A woman staggered over table legs and admiring glares of the German soldiers, apologising to the old man behind the counter for being as late as she was.

I counted down the second to twelve thirty-seven, Jules' eyes boring into my forehead as I did so. As quickly as the girl had flown into the café, twelve thirty-seven came and went.

"He is late?" Jules asked, impatiently.

I said nothing, but tried to nod my head in some sort of sign that I was still with it.

"Then we go, now," he muttered, with a sense of urgency so strong that I thought I would have to drag him back down into his seat.

I supposed he didn't want to be arrested by the Germans any more than I did.

"Wait," I said sharply. "Leave it a few more seconds, then we'll go. Slowly."

I downed the last bit of my now rancid coffee as I

checked myself over, readying to leave. Jules did the same.

"Alright then," I said, "Let's go."

Just as I was about to get up and kick my chair backwards, the door swung open again, a man filling the frame that was almost as wide as the door itself. His hair was dark and unkempt, his mucky face and hands doing nothing for my overall impression of the man.

"Stop," Jules said, quite loudly. "That's him."

"Him?" I asked, looking him up and down as he pulled a bag from his back. "Jules, he looks nothing like the person you described earlier on."

"We were only boys back then."

"No one changes that much."

"I'd recognise *le blaireau* from a mile off."

"*Le blaireau?*" I repeated, making sure I had heard correctly.

He looked me dead in the eyes, as the man began to stumble towards us, with less admiring looks than the young girl had received. "The badger," he stated, as the man pulled up a chair next to us and dumped the bag at his feet.

He too was wearing the same uniform as the other workers, a blue jumpsuit that had faded with age, covered almost head to foot in grease and grime.

He motioned to the café owner for some coffee and growled into the small air that we shared between us.

"Put these on. Identity cards are in your pockets.

Do what I do and don't engage with the Germans. Keep your heads down. We'll be going in with my lads, so hopefully your faces will get lost in amongst them."

The girl plonked the badger's coffee down, which he threw down his neck quicker than anything I had seen before.

"Come on, we haven't got all day."

He chucked some notes onto the table and rose from it, making for the door and the waiting cloud of cigarette smoke that lingered outside.

Jules and I, on the other hand, milled around for a second or two, before heading out to the restroom one at a time, to change from the two, unexceptional civilians, into two greasy, invisible factory workers.

"You all ready?" Jules asked me, as he waved a goodbye to the café owner and apologized to a group of German NCOs, as he was forced to step over their outstretched legs.

"Yeah," I muttered under my breath, so quietly that I did not think he could hear, as we tumbled from the café and, in a group of about seven boisterous factory workers, made our way to the target.

17

The second that I made eye contact with the jumpy German soldier on guard duty, I knew that I had made a mistake. I wanted to check him out, to see where he was looking and whether the sentries here were switched on enough to notice two completely clean and never before seen men, in amongst their comrades of dirtied faces and filthy palms.

It was a risky game, but one that I was hoping would give me the upper hand. But, as the soldier pointed to me, in the centre of the gaggle of men who waddled through the checkpoint, I realised quite quickly that it was a foolish game to be playing.

I couldn't quite make out his voice, as he pushed the others out the way and in through the factory gates. He wasn't concerned with any of them, he was totally focused on the man who had been locked in a staring contest with him, and he didn't like to lose.

His voice was immature and weak, but it was not

something that I would make fun of him for, as the rifle barrel that twitched over his shoulder told me that he was taking this far more seriously than I was.

Obliging, I handed over my papers, which he snatched from my hand with long, curling fingernails, without taking his gaze from my face. He studied them for a fleeting second, before choosing to stare at me for a few seconds longer, to see if I would crack.

Underneath the surface I wanted to burst into tears, to shatter into a thousand pieces in amongst the shame of my foolishness. But, on the outside, as I had been taught to do over many months, I maintained a cool façade of indignance but equally of confidence.

I turned away from him briefly, to look over his shoulder at the concerned faces that were glaring back at me, from Jules and Peintre's contact, whose name I had not been able to get, and might never now know.

They carried on regardless, as I would have expected them to, if I was banned from the grounds of the factory, or arrested, then at least Jules would hopefully get a good look around and with any luck report back with his findings.

As the German continued to test my patience, I could not help but look up at the long, sweeping windows that looked down on the front courtyard that the others were now disappearing through.

Somewhere, behind a dirtied glass pane, made even more opaque by the glinting sunlight, I imagined the grey figure of Captain Murky, his lips snarling as he applied the pressure more and more to our circuit.

Which was why it was all the more stupid of me to try and toy with the guard who now stood in my way.

"Are you a new worker?" he asked, in heavily accented French.

"No, I have been here a good many months," I said, risking a smirk and a carefree attitude that only an agreeable employee could adopt.

His lips tightened, as his gut told him that there was something wrong with the man that he had stopped, but his inexperience was stopping him from working out what it was. Nervously, he looked behind him, Jules just managing to turn around in time for the young sentry to catch the back of his head as he disappeared into a large, warehouse door.

I imagined that he was looking for one of his fellow countrymen, to check the card he had in front of him and eye up the suspicious chap. But my imagination told me, it could also have been out of a wariness that an SS officer had recently turned up, and he didn't want to look a fool in front of him if he waved through a dubious character.

"I have not seen you here before."

I snorted through my nose gently, forcing a wide smile across my face, before letting it retreat rapidly as if only just realising that he was being totally serious.

"Well, I have seen you here before," I stated as confidently as I could muster. "Every day in fact. Don't they give you lot a day off?"

Something twitched in his face and I wondered if I had amused him, or simply spat on his face. I let my chuckle linger for a moment, my heart rate thumping harder than before as I realised that the next two seconds would be decisive.

The sweat that began to roll from under my hairline started to gather pace and, if he was not going to let me through in the next second or so, he would spot it as it ran towards my eyes. And I was convinced that would mean the game was up.

His hand twitched, as he caressed the butt of his rifle. He was thinking about it.

But then, as if suddenly having a change of heart, he threw my identity card from one hand to the other and passed it back to me ceremoniously.

"I see so many faces I don't know who I have seen before and who I have not."

"It must be nice to see one that is smiling, no?" I said as I took my card and paced past him and into the factory. I grimaced, waiting for the call that would halt my progression across the courtyard, but nothing came. He had either misunderstood what it was that I had said or had genuinely found some sort of amusement from it.

I didn't turn around to work out which it was.

I struggled to hide my true emotions as I thundered across the courtyard, aiming for the door that I had seen the others disappear into. A few other workers milled around nearby, some smoking, others just taking in the warm sunbeams, but not one of them paid a great deal of attention to me. One of them even waved a greeting to me from across the way. Either they all knew who I was and had no qualms about me forcing them into unemployment, or they were just blind as a bat.

My legs burned awfully by the time that I found the others, who had tucked themselves away just on the inside of the door, and had watched the whole encounter from the safety of the long shadows created by the glowing sun, that kissed our contact's face as he welcomed me in.

"I'm Cluzet," he said, slapping me on the back. "That there is Diehl. He doesn't have a clue what is going on half the time. I am convinced he is a drunk."

"He doesn't know who works here and who doesn't," one of our group muttered. "Diehl stopped Cluzet here last week because apparently he'd never seen him before."

"I've been working here for the last fifteen years. I've been in through those gates every day since the occupation started," Cluzet said, shrugging, wiping his spectacles unsuccessfully on his oily rags and placing them on his face.

It was only as Cluzet began to give us a tour of the place that I realised what a close call I had just encountered. A wave of nausea almost overpowered me, and the strength in my legs diminished in a matter of seconds.

My face suddenly felt cold and I felt the blood drain from it from top to bottom. Within about thirty seconds, most of my blood was in the soles of my feet, as I realised that if Diehl had been switched on, I could have been shot on the spot.

I couldn't afford another close call like that one.

Jules sidled up next to me and leant into my ear.

"I suppose that rules you out on the night then?"

I snapped out of the slippery pit that I was falling deeper into, the blood shooting up from my feet with verve. Within half a second, it was boiling again, lighting up my face like the side of a London bus.

"Why not? If anything, that means that I am the perfect person to lead on this."

Jules scoffed, inciting a feeling of dislike towards him for the first time since I had met him.

I felt like I had to justify myself, but also keep my voice under very strict controls.

"He's seen me. He's waved me through. With any luck he will remember my face. If we plan it to take place on a night that he is on guard duty, then he'll wave us all through. What just happened there makes our job ten times easier on the night."

Jules shrugged, as if to say that he would defer judgement until the others could debate what would happen, but I knew that my voice would tower over Jules'. It wasn't arrogance, but a deep-rooted confidence, that had been instilled in me in the Highlands. I had been trained, Jules had not.

Besides, I knew that Diehl had a weakness; he liked a drink. That could help us out no end further along the line.

"There are three main workshop floors," Cluzet

started as he turned and walked backwards, his arms outstretched. "This is the boring workshop, where we use the jig borers to put holes in various parts for later in the production process."

I watched as men manipulated howling machinery into flat sheets of steel, sparks flying up everywhere and dancing across the backs of the men's arms. It was clear now why so many of the men had scorch marks on the blue boiler suits, or small burn marks on their hands and arms.

"The assembly plant is directly overhead. Decidedly less boisterous," he said, raising his voice to a shout to be heard over the din. "We also have a small gas producing plant, which may or may not be of interest to you."

I zoned out from what he was saying, partly as it was becoming increasingly difficult to hear what he was saying the closer we got to the noisiest machinery, but also because I already knew all of this.

I had studied the plans that Peintre had given us for hours, until I knew that I could have walked around the factory in my sleep and known where everything was. I had needed to, in case we had not been able to gain entry until the night of the attack, if that had been the case then there would still have been a chance of making a success out of it all.

But, as a bonus, Peintre had directed us towards Cluzet, who was now proudly giving us a tour of all the main features of the factory, helping me to work out where slight changes had been made, or finding darkened corners that would not show on the building plans that we had been given.

I focused on one man in particular, as I watched him at a large lathe, allowing it to spin and form a large piece of metal into what must have been some kind of mechanical shaft.

I had seen one working before, back when I was still training, but this one was different, as it was almost twice the size.

The one that I had seen previously had been built specifically for people like me; those who were learning to blow stuff up.

It was one of the only things that I had taken to in training with any real enthusiasm, purely because I realised, I was pretty good at rendering things unserviceable with nothing more than a little bit of plastic explosive.

This lathe would take a little bit more plastic than the one that I had learned to blow up, but I was confident that the machine would be nothing more than an impractical twisted mess of steel by the time that I had finished with it.

As we continued to look around the factory, taking in all the other machines and what they were being used for, I realised that I wasn't able to look at anything to marvel at the innovation or technological advancement any longer.

All I could think of now when I saw something like a lathe, jig-borer or the sand dryers, was how best to blow the thing up and, preferably, using the least amount of explosive as possible. I had learnt quickly that it wasn't just a case of making the biggest bang, or making it appear all twisted, but it was about destroying the vital parts, the parts that would take an age to source replacements for, or too fiddly to even attempt.

It was those smaller things that I was studying closely now.

"Where are the Germans?" Jules asked, as we were shown into a far quieter room, where the clanking metal and shouts of men were dampened considerably. I continued to try and piece together the plans that we had been given with what I was now seeing and managed to work out where we were, based on the overhead pipes that carried cleaner air into the factory.

"We don't see them in here. They aren't allowed to smoke. Besides, it's far too noisy for them to spend a long time in here. It's why we can talk freely."

The noise grew dimmer as Cluzet continued to show us around in silence, noticing a long time ago that we were not interested in his salesman-like patter about how many engines the factory could churn out in a day, but seemingly found impossible now under the management of the Germans.

"I have something that might be of particular interest to you. Out here."

He opened a door, heavy and resistant, that led into an alleyway of sorts.

"This," he said, extending his arms down the

narrow path that had a high wall on one side and the factory on the other, "is your escape route."

He paced down it a little more. "And a rather nice surprise for you as well."

We turned a corner, where we were faced with a great hunk of metal, an impressive amount of tubes and carburettors clearly sticking out from it wherever possible. It was at least eight feet tall and towered over the three of us as we stood staring at it.

"This is the main emergency generator. The bombing hasn't done much to the factory, but it has had some effect on the power that we receive. The Germans have put this in to kick in when that drops out. It has the ability to power the entire factory for up to twelve hours at a time. It gives the Germans time to get the main power reconnected.

"If you can destroy this," he whispered, "this whole place could be in darkness for weeks."

I tried to smile back at the Frenchman, whose grin was so menacing that I was beginning to fear for my life.

"That down there will be your bid for freedom. There's a dip in the wall. Only about three metres high. As long as you're travelling lighter than when you came in, you should be able to get over it."

He winked, with a sinister glint in his eye. Something told me that I would do well to have Cluzet by my side on the night that we would go in.

18

I was able to simply eat up the clouds as they raced towards my face, the sun just dipping below them and casting a wide net of weakened orange across the entire skyscape. I basked in the peacefulness of it all, despite the roaring Merlin that was strapped in front of me. This was surely the closest to heaven that a mere mortal could ever get.

There was no one around me, I was the only living thing for miles around and the freedom that I felt I had whilst in possession of those controls was unfathomable. There was something so special about it, being higher than the birds, with no manmade stain anywhere in sight.

I pushed the throttle marginally further forward, my head jumping backwards slightly at the increased acceleration. My shortness of breath was down to nothing more than pure exhilaration as I endeavoured to discover any and every cloud that lingered over this small patch of England.

Every now and then, I would pass through a cloud, flying level from one side to the next, something I had been explicitly forbidden from doing, but the splash of light that glanced off the glass of the cockpit upon exiting was truly wonderful.

I remembered that first, truly solo, flight in the Hurricane as if I was still experiencing it now. It was the first time that I had ever been entrusted to fly without anyone by my side, no one over comms to tell me that I should do this and shouldn't do that. It was only me.

Slowly, the dials and switches gradually disappeared, until all I could focus on was the fantastically burnt orange sky, and the wistful clouds that I danced through at over two hundred miles an hour.

It was the fastest that I had ever travelled and yet, in the Hurrie, everything felt as comfortable and smooth as if I was doing less than a hundred. I longed to be able to look behind me and watch as the wisping clouds were obliterated as I charged through them, but realised that staring dead ahead was just as rewarding.

The hairs on the backs of my arms stood to attention, the tears gushing to my eyes as I pulled hard on the paddle in between my legs and climbed as high as I dared.

I shot through yet another cloud on my way to the moon, as the exhalation of exhilaration turned quickly into a chuckle, and just as quickly, a full-body laugh. My body shook as I grinned so wide that my oxygen mask began to unbuckle itself.

"Woohoo!" I screeched at the top of my lungs as I lurched round into an inverted flight, my head skimming the tops of the clouds and my feet the highest things for miles around.

"Woo!" I continued, until almost completely out of breath, before righting myself to its natural order and allowing the blood to rush away from my burgeoning skull.

I navigated into a steep bank, increasing the revs as I did so and feeling the power of the mighty Merlin begin to thunder across the wooden airframe of the Hurricane. Confidently, I held my turn, even when the nausea at the sheer speed I was travelling at began to press into my chest.

My laughter and cheering had died down into nothing more than short, sharp breaths, as the pure elation at flying in such a wonderful machine began to take its toll on my physical wellbeing.

My emotions were so full of a pure love and happiness, that I wished that someone was there alongside me to experience it. At first, I thought I would want Grace, my wife alongside me, but I quickly realised that there was someone else who would have taken a greater joy out of my own happiness; my father.

He would have loved it up there, away from the hustle and bustle of life and the sheer insanity of man. He had seen plenty of it before, but up there, where the pale clouds simply dissipated at the first hint of resistance, I knew he would have been able to find a peace.

The billowing clouds kept on coming, like a spewing volcano, while I put the aircraft into a shallow dive, levelling off for a few seconds so that I could take in the pure, brilliant white of the latest cloud's internal organs.

The light began to stutter and waiver as I left one cloud and entered another, allowing me just a quick glimpse at my fuel gauge. It was lingering somewhere just over halfway, which meant that it was time to head for home, unless I wanted a very angry Flight Sergeant barking at me, while also trying not to end up on an insubordination charge.

I edged the paddle forward and within half a second, I was below the clouds once again. It had done nothing but rain for the past few days, but I had been graced with a fleeting break in the poor weather, that meant I had been able to fly solo for the first time.

Everything below me though was slightly subdued, a darker colour to the fields and trees that stood guard on the earth below. Nothing seemed to move, just a damp, dark world trying to dry itself out in the last few minutes of fading sunshine.

There was a chill as I got closer to the surface of the earth, one that I hadn't experienced in the half an hour or so that I had spent above the clouds. The hairs that had stood upright through pure joy and elation now did so to catch any kind of warmth that they could, and the pimples of my skin rose up as a shiver shot through my body.

The world seemed impossibly darker here, as if the sun had been staying awake just long enough for me to enjoy myself, but had now retired to bed.

Shadows slowly rolled over the fields below, plunging everything into a sweeping darkness.

"It's going to rain again," I said into my mask, trying to comfort myself as one does when convinced there are monsters under the bed. "Best get back soon."

I began circling over the landscape, taking in everything that I could use as some sort of waypoint, pulling my map onto my lap.

This was the very purpose that I had been sent up, to ensure that I could still navigate having been disorientated by being above the clouds, but it was harder than I thought it would have been.

I kept my wings level and throttled down slightly, so that I didn't accidentally find myself somewhere over France in the blink of an eye.

I looked down at my lap, my gloved finger tracing where it was I thought I could have been, before sliding it over to the airfield where all my fun had started.

Adjusting my mask over my face, allowing a blast of cool air to relieve the perspiration that had formed up on the inside, I saw something dance fantastically over my right shoulder.

I craned my neck to see if I could see anything, but there was nothing there. Instead, I looked dead ahead once again, just as I caught something zip over my left wing.

As soon as I had realised what it was, the bullets had found their target, and the soft thump as rounds ripped into the flesh of the Hurricane soon filled my ears.

I dived, harder than I perhaps should have done, trying to remember everything that I had learned in the classroom about what to do when a 109 appeared on your tail.

Full throttle. Fine pitch. Full left rudder. Full left and full forward stick.

I held it for a few seconds as I barrelled into a horrific spin.

My eyes felt as though they were about to push through the back of my skull, and I could feel blood rushing to try and fill them as I was blinded by the sheer weight of the force that pushed down on my head.

I began to panic as I heard the rounds continue to flitter on the wings of the Hurricane, ripping huge chunks out of my precious machine.

"Why are you still on me? How are you still there?!" I screamed at the top of my lungs; my limbs now so heavy that I was finding it difficult to pull the Hurricane from the negative spin.

Blindly, I fumbled around, trying to go through the motions of pulling myself out of the spin before I collided with the ground. As I did so, my eyesight returned, the dampened yellow of a freshly threshed, recently rained upon field filled my vision.

I braced for impact.

"JOHNNY."

I took the glass that was pushed under my nose, drank, and grimaced, forcing it down.

It shocked my body for a moment, before allowing it to warm my blood once again and bring me back to my senses.

"Same dream?" Mike asked as he backed away from me cautiously, as I shuffled around in the chair. My clothes were sodden.

They clung to every inch of my skin as if they had somehow become fused together in the short time that I had been asleep.

"Yeah," I whispered back to him, my throat hoarse either from the fear of the dream or the strong drink that Jules had managed to find from somewhere.

I noticed quite quickly that a plethora of faces stared back at me, wary of the ticking time bomb that I had become. I tried to pull myself together for them, but especially for one face in particular.

Georges pootled up towards me and sat at my

feet, clearly understanding the warning signs that I, as a mad man, was giving off.

"I have nightmares too," he said, unfazed by my spasming body, as he pushed a small four-wheeled toy around the floor.

"I know," I growled, far more viciously than I ought. "You've told me before," I tried to force out something that resembled a smile but could only muster a slight twitch of my lips.

Mike called Georges to him, to engage with him some more and get him away from me. It was becoming impossible for me to hide my emotions, I could even see it in the wide, awe-filled eyes of young Georges as he was dragged across the floor.

He could tell, despite his young years, that I had dismissed him forcefully. It was not because I did not believe him that I had done so, but because I thought mine were more affecting than his, more important, which, in his world at least, was not the case.

I closed my eyes as I tried to bring everything back down to its normal levels. My ears continued to thump methodically as the sounds of the rounds continued to hit my wingtips, until they grew louder and longer, like a percussion instrument.

"Shush. Listen in," Andrew said, as I realised that the bullets had become a drum, thumping out the start of the *Messages Personnels.*

Everyone stood upright as the man, crackled and weak, began to speak.

"Ici Londres! Ici Londres! Les Français parlent aux Français…"

He continued to speak, above the racket that had started to sound as the Germans tried their utmost to jam the signal, almost always failing. That night was no different.

"…avant de commencer, veuillez écouter quelques messages personnels…"

The defiant voice continued unperturbed, as he began to spew all kinds of obscure statements and humorous anecdotes. It was clear to everyone that these were coded messages but, without the context and the necessary codes, the Germans had no hope in deciphering them, or understanding what they meant.

I was convinced that well over half of them were meant for no one other than the newsreader, who must have taken great enjoyment in broadcasting statements like '*ta mère a pris une baignoire sale à l'église.*'

Your mother took a dirty bathtub to church.

I let the others listen in, knowing full well that they would not miss the message, even if I did. I kept an ear out, catching phrases here and there, as the whine of a failing jammer continued to scream out into the room.

"Sylvie est grande mais parfois non."

That was what they had been waiting for.

I sat in the chair, biting my knuckle hard as I tried to ignore the sopping clothes that I sat in, fearful that consciously thinking about it would make me perspire even more.

"Well, that's that then," Mike announced slapping his thigh.

"Tomorrow night," Andrew said with a smile on his face, lurching towards Mike and shaking hands.

"Just as well. Your four-week time limit runs out tomorrow," Jules said, with a sobering effect on the two congratulating each other.

"Nothing will go wrong. We've prepared well," Mike said, rising from his chair and pacing the floor, ruffling Georges' hair as he did so. "Don't worry Jules. After tomorrow night, you won't have to worry about any more raids. This is going to start a new war. One where there aren't as many innocent casualties."

Jules turned away violently and scampered through the door.

"What's got into him?" Mike asked the room, shrugging.

"Shush!" Christopher mumbled, waving at everyone to take their seats. He scooted in closer to the wireless set and practically cradled the thing towards his ear as he sat on the floor.

"What?"

"Shush!"

Mike did as he was told, with a bemused look on his face as everyone around him told him to keep his mouth shut.

"La porte du jardin est peinte en rose."

"Ah! Aha!" he suddenly exclaimed, as the broadcaster slowly came to the end of his evening session. "*Rose! Rose!*"

He began to screech, standing unsteadily on his feet, his wide thighs threatening to buckle under the weight of his top half. He stretched to the ceiling, which was still a long way off for him, before linking his fingers behind his head.

"The garden gate is painted pink. What's that got to do with us?"

"It has nothing to do with you!" he babbled. "It has *everything* to do with me!"

"Spit it out, man. What are you going on about?"

"It is painted pink! I am a father! To a little girl!"

I snorted audibly, as my stomach lurched from one side to the other, my mind having a battle with itself over whether to feel happy for the man, or a burning jealously.

I settled with the happiness, as my jealousy was borne from a nightmare which I could not wish upon anyone.

19

Mike had never been one for needing an excuse to have any kind of celebration, and so, by the time I was able to garner enough energy to lift my weary and burdensome limbs up the stairs to bed, a small party was gathering pace below.

There was a little bit of music, that filtered through the floorboards occasionally, just above the din of the three remaining men downstairs as they basked in one another's happiness.

That was the thing about people who were always looking over their shoulder, worried about what the next day might bring, if someone around you had a smile on their face, then it did you no harm to wear one back. As you didn't quite know if you would still be able to do the same tomorrow.

It was a feeling that I had often shared, but the message that we had received had not filled me with the hope of changing the war, in the way that it had for everyone else.

I was worried, petrified even, and it was in no small part down to the looming shadow of the dream that I had lingering over me.

It was not the end of the world I told myself as, if I was to die tomorrow, then there would be no other soul who would ever experience one my nightmares ever again. I took an ounce of hope from the fact that that had been the last one that would ever race through my mind.

My aching brain and weary eyes were so affected by the exhausting dream, that I almost clattered into the back of Jules as he edged his way out of Georges bedroom. Gently, he closed the door, before jumping as he saw me standing directly behind him like some sort of silent assassin.

"*Jean.* Ah, I didn't hear you."

"Sorry, Jules. I-I didn't mean to. Goodnight," I said, taking in the sight of the floorboards as I traipsed towards my room at the back of the house.

"Erm, Jean," he whispered loudly, as if trying to call me back. "Georges. I know you care for him. But when he says he has the nightmares too…"

"I know. I'm sorry Jules. I will talk to him about it in the morning. I just couldn't stomach it tonight."

"He means it, Jean. He has the nightmares. Because he…he saw them first. It is why it is so remarkable that he is the way he is. He was the one to find…"

"Jules?" I said, stepping closer to him and catching the first tears as they fell to the floor with a soft plink.

"You promise that these air raids will stop? If you succeed tomorrow?"

"I can almost guarantee it," I said boldly, with a hint of deception rumbling somewhere in the pit of my stomach. I did not like lying, but especially to a man like Jules, who had done nothing more than help us.

"Georges he-he…When the bombers came over…We found him in the rubble the next morning. He was still holding Céleste's hand."

"Who is Céleste?" I asked tentatively, craning my head to try and find his eyes under his bowed head.

"She *was* my wife. Georges' mother. He held her hand through it all. She must have died hours before. He saw it all."

I suddenly felt quite sick, and overwhelmingly guilty. I had loved the child but had equally been quick to dismiss him as fast as I could on account of the fact that I could not see past my own situation and sorrow. The boy had lost his mother which, at such a young age, was a travesty beyond words.

"Jules," I said, resting both hands on his shoulders, the sweat lifting from my body and the strength returning to my muscles. "I will make sure that we see this through. For you, and for Georges. With any luck, it'll mean that the rest of Georges' experience of this war will be limited to just the rationing."

I smiled warily, as he sucked up the final few tears that were already out of the ducts.

"I know you will. I know. I trust you. Thank you."

I squeezed his shoulders tightly and patted his arms as I let him stand on his own two feet again.

"Goodnight, Jean."

"Goodnight, Jules."

I turned and headed for bed, the incredible pressure that was already resting on my shoulders now taking on the form of a weight that was three times as heavy.

I could feel sorry for Georges all I liked on that night. But, as soon as morning rolled round, it would be time to push his innocent little face from my mind, and make sure the Germans paid for what they did to his mother.

20

The long, drawn-out shadows that flickered along the courtyard floor were mesmerising, as the men that cast them moved away, the darkness dancing like a flame. The walls that surrounded the courtyard allowed little of the late afternoon sun to conquer its perimeter and, as I stood in a newly-formed shadow in one of the corners, smoking, a chill passed over me that pricked at the hairs on my arms.

I rolled the sleeves of my boiler suit down to my wrists, resisting the urge to shiver and rub my limbs, instead occupying myself with the faces of the men who were passing me by without a second glance.

All around faces came and went, a few that I recognised, the majority that I had never before seen. Soon though, I watched as faces that I knew well began to form from the shadows, featureless to begin with, but more rounded and defined as we got closer to each other.

It was a comfort to know that I wasn't alone, and that I would have someone to both rely on, as well as avoid letting down. I had always found that more of a driving force than anything else, the fear of knowing that someone else wasn't able to do their job, simply because you had failed to do yours. It was something that I was petrified of, as I padded across the courtyard, like a prisoner, taking his exercise out in the yard.

My footsteps were silent as I glided across the ground, the plimsoles on my feet cushioning the noise that was so emanant on all the other workers' feet.

My toes twitched around inside as I excitedly tried to get some sort of feeling back into them, the narrow, constricting nature of the plimsoles rubbing at my skin and making them raw. All the same, the electricity that pulsated through the tips of my toes was apparent around the whole of my body, as my thoughts turned to my evening's work.

There was an ecstasy, that was only kept in check by the almost paralytic fear that something was going to go horribly wrong, the two balancing each other out nicely so that I remained in possession of a calm mind.

It was what was stopping the erraticism of my thoughts, as I coolly made my way through the steps that we had planned to take, and any eventuality that I could think of. By visualising everything, from being compromised by some Germans to stitched up by another factory worker, I had a simmering confidence that we were going to succeed.

I flicked my cigarette away with a large exhale of breath, as I attempted to ground myself once more. Dogfights had only ever been lost because of the sheer arrogance of the loser, as my CO had once reminded us all.

I wasn't in the air now, or in possession of a rapid weapon of war, but the principles applied all the same. I had to keep myself in check.

There was a lot riding on this, I found myself muttering internally, far too much to allow arrogance to be our stumbling block.

A whole town, just the other side of the wall that was now forcing its shadow upon me, relied on what was in the hands of just a few men on the inside. If only they had known, if only I could just have been able to tell them to hold on a little bit more, and someone would do something about all the bombs. They deserved it.

They had been battered and bruised, decimated and destroyed, hundreds of bombers dropping thousands of pounds worth of explosives. All those endless nights of terror, hoping to be ended by a handful of men and a couple of pounds of explosives.

On paper, none of it seemed quite right. But we had done our research.

They would know soon enough, I told myself, as the urge to scream and shout to all of the inhabitants of *Besançon* grew stronger once more. They would hear the explosions and the confusion of the Germans and know that someone was fighting back for them. I had to wipe the smile from my face, as some of the departing workers were starting to give me odd looks.

I twisted and turned as I slithered in and out the tidal wave of workers that were now pouring from every door that I could see. I battled against the tide as I made it to the centre, where we had all agreed to meet before heading back inside.

It had been a long day; a full working day just like any other employee, only we were going to be putting in some rather serious overtime.

I looked at the faces around me, to take in the expressions of the men that would be my safety net for the rest of the evening. Five of us in total; three Brits, two Frenchmen. But, our outward appearance, so far, showed one of unity and shared experience.

Uncharacteristically, Mike looked the most apprehensive, his bottom lip disappearing inside his mouth as he chewed away at the dry and cracked skin that had formed on the surface. There had been no time to source some water for any of us in the last few hours and, even if we had, the nerves were enough to make even the moistest of throats bone dry.

Without saying another word Cluzet, the foreman who had given us a tour around the facilities a week or so ago, led our onslaught against the tide of greasy-faced men, as we fought against them to get back into the factory.

His slightly generous proportions meant that he

waddled rather than walked, a limp on one side making him seem rather comical. Nevertheless, he had been as serious as anything when it had come down to planning the intricacies of our op.

He had been the one to convince us that working the full day on the factory floor, rather than resting up, would be far more beneficial to us. The Germans, unsurprisingly, were more wary of those coming in later on in the day than those that had been there since morning.

Besides, it gave us another opportunity to get up close and personal to the machines that were causing so much havoc in the way of engine building, and to learn the layout of some of the passageways and corridors without the threat of German interference.

We had spent hours with Cluzet, going over everything that might have been a stumbling block to us, including whether or not there would be other workers around at that time of night.

"There are always people working in that factory," he had said rather confidently. "But they won't get in your way. They hate anyone who makes them work those kinds of hours. And they will only be too happy to help those who want to put a stop to them."

It didn't sit perfectly with me, as all it would take would be one disgruntled worker, who valued his wages more than he did scoring against the Germans and the whole thing would come tumbling down around us.

"We wait here," Cluzet announced, lighting up a

cigarette and leaning against the wall, surveying the scene as the final few remnants began to drip from the factory and trudge home.

"How was Christopher?" Andrew said, wriggling over to me and putting a foot up on the wall behind him.

"Fine," I answered, thinking of the little man as he sat outside the café. "He seemed quite alright actually. All smiles and waves."

Andrew scoffed at the thought, but with an element of frustration that he knew that I was telling the truth. Christopher had helped us tremendously by talking to Peintre, but other than that, he had not been much help at all.

He had been placed in the café, across from the main entrance to the factory and he was no doubt sipping at a cup of coffee as he watched the men stream from the main gate, as we had just seen them go a few minutes before.

It was his job to wait outside, armed with nothing but a Sten gun hidden under his long jacket, and the courage that I hoped was somewhere in his blood.

"I only hope we don't need him. He's a terrible shot."

"As long as he doesn't somehow hit us, I don't care where he fires the thing."

It was just as well that Christopher's job was not marksmanship, but chaos making, kicking out a magazine of nine millimetre the second that he suspected something was going awry inside.

I was pleased also with the fact that he was not with us on the inside of the perimeter, as he had not filled me with the greatest confidence in what I had seen of him so far.

"Tell me, is he good at anything?" I asked, leaning into Andrew.

"He makes a blinding beef wellington," he said, mockingly. "Not a lot of hope of you seeing one of those. I haven't seen a cow in weeks."

I scoffed, as the courtyard began to empty, and the large barn style door about ten yards away became more visible. It was there that we would start our little adventure, all we needed to do was bide our time a little bit more. The Germans were doing their last sweep of the day, to make sure that nothing was missing from the factory floor and in a worker's pocket instead.

I recalled the look on Christopher's face upon hearing the news that he was a new father to a tiny child, and I could not but feel happy for the man who had caused me so much anxiety. There was something about the tears in his eyes, the pure joy etched onto his skin that made it impossible not to be.

But it was that happiness that was causing me great discomfort, as it would mean that his judgement would have been even more clouded than before. That on top of the small fact that he was a conscientious objector.

For his sake, as well as my own, I hoped earnestly that his interference would not come into play tonight, and that the next half an hour or so would play out smoothly, and he would be able to return back to the safehouse and begin to prepare for our exfiltration.

At the thought of the carnage that could ensue as we tried to enter the factory properly, I felt for my own weapon.

We could not risk having something like a Sten gun on our person, despite its ease of concealment, and instead had an ugly looking thing that disguised itself as a Webley self-loading pistol.

I had fired them once or twice before, reliably informed by an instructor that it was a pistol used by the Royal Navy.

"Famous for using their sidearms," one chipper voice had chimed in sarcastically at the time.

But now, I found myself relying heavily on it for my life, its loud echoing report and its huge recoil the only thing that could stand between success and failure. If all else went south, then I would have to press it into my own mouth, something that I had reluctantly practiced doing the night before.

I thought of Georges, as we waited for the seconds to tick by and for the Germans to emerge from the barn door, and what it was he was doing right at that moment. He was with an auntie of some description, and I could only hope that he kept his small infant mouth closed, not breathing a word about the strange men that had been in his home for several weeks.

I had no other option but to trust the small boy, as

I had done with so many other people in a far better position to betray us. But I could not help but feel the awesome weight of responsibility on my shoulders as I thought of the prospect of an air-raid free life for the child.

He had already seen enough of them for his little eyes.

Gently, and without wanting to alert any of the others to my actions, I began to feel each of my pockets, one by one, gripping hard on the solid outlines as they sat in the lining of my trousers, and one in my breast pocket.

Undoing the button on it, I felt around the cold casing of one of the mines that would hopefully bring an end to the misery of the inhabitants of *Besançon*.

All I needed to do now was live long enough to plant it.

21

We all tried to ignore the three German soldiers as they emerged from the factory floor, allowing Cluzet to take control and do the looking for us. But it was difficult, and, on more than one occasion, my wandering eyes stared at them as they stalked across the courtyard, their field caps neatly on their heads.

"Right then, seeing as you all want to get going. It looks like we're clear," Cluzet muttered, his youthful eyes glinting as he spoke to us all. He seemed like a relaxed man, but he looked at us all in turn, with such solemnity that I felt the weight of responsibility slap me in the face.

"I must thank you for doing this. We have been hoping for a moment like this for a very long time. Good luck to you all."

"Thank you, Cluzet," Mike mumbled back. "Good luck to you too."

"Shall we get a move on then?" I interjected,

before the two of them could shake hands and embrace. We had worked so hard to remain undetected that to falter now would be a travesty.

Suddenly my heart began to pound, and I could feel every ounce of my hot blood surging around my veins, my neck throbbing with excitement. My limbs trembled, in a good way, as my body started preparing itself for what was about to happen.

I felt ready to go, to run and leap over the nine-foot wall that surrounded the courtyard, completely unaided. If things went wrong, I was sure that I could outrun the Germans, all the way to the Swiss border.

I was fired up.

It was a sensation that panicked me as much as it did excite. I was pleased that I felt the way I did, and not cowering in some corner somewhere anxiously awaiting all the things that could go wrong. It made a change to how I normally felt.

But, equally, I was concerned that in my dynamism and eagerness, I would do something that would plunge the entire operation into doubt. It was in this kind of state of mind that people did things wrong, getting themselves killed, or even worse, the rest of the team.

It was that possibility of living, while everyone else perished, that filled me with an overwhelming guilt before anything had even happened. Hoping desperately that the fear of letting everyone down would dampen my enthusiasm, I nodded to Mike so that he knew I was ready.

It was not a normal experience of war, a war that very few people had been through in all the millennia of conflict.

For centuries, warriors and soldiers had charged into battle with blood surging and hearts pumping, in much the same way that mine was as we stood in the courtyard. But, for our war, the opposite was necessary for success.

We needed to remain calm, level-headed and able to make rational decisions in the heat of the moment. To do so would allow for a greater chance of success and for better odds of not being noticed by the enemy, who were everywhere.

I thought back to a calmer, quieter place, to return to some sort of docility that would assist in my endeavour.

Before long, I was stretched out in a cool, flowing stream in the heart of Cornwall, hiding beneath the canopy of autumnal leaves that had only just started to crisp and brown. It had seemed so long ago now that I could hardly remember names, but faces still lingered for a moment or two.

As we staggered towards the large door, I could see the outline of the old Victorian farmhouse, that had become my sanctuary shortly after I had seen the lifeless bodies of my infant son and wife.

The sudden diversion in my thoughts caused me to cut away and focus on keeping one foot in front of the other, following the bobbing heads of my fellow saboteurs.

Everything was going swimmingly, I thought, as I managed to complete six or seven steps without falling flat on my face.

Out of the blue, a short, sharp bark ruptured the pitter-patter of footsteps and we all ground to a halt, like a well-rehearsed drill team.

There was no opportunity to breathe and my heart ached as it held on to its urgency to beat one last time. Everything stopped in our world as we waited to see what the next instruction would be.

Despite the fact that we had already stopped in the exact spot we had been told, the voice called out for a second time.

"Stop!"

I turned, the others backing me up by doing the exact same. I could feel more than one person feeling around in their pockets for their weapons. It was not unheard of, Cluzet had said, for the Germans to suddenly search anyone they liked. It particularly happened when they were bored or frustrated.

If they were to do that to us, we were going to need to call on Christopher and his Sten gun, after all.

Diehl was standing on the other side of the courtyard to us, not all that far away from the entrance gate that we had passed through earlier in the day.

He swayed ever so slightly, as if there was a gentle breeze on that side of the factory, and he brushed shoulders gently with two of the soldiers who stood either side of them. Two more sidled up alongside them, until they formed one mass of hideous German soldier.

"What's he got in his hands?" Mike breathed amongst us.

"Which one?" Cluzet muttered back.

"I'm hardly going to point at him, am I Cluzet? Obviously the one holding that thing in his arms."

"I don't know," Cluzet replied, unperturbed by the aggression that had hissed from Mike's lips.

"Just be grateful it isn't weapons. All their rifles are still on their shoulders."

"That's something."

"*Fußball!*" Diehl screamed at the top of his lungs, as the man next to him dropped a shadow, before volleying it towards us. As the football sailed through the air, Diehl guffawed and screamed again. "*Ein Spiel!*"

We stood in dumbfounded silence for a moment, not one of us wanting to be the first to move and make some kind of fatal error.

"A football match?" Andrew said, disbelief apparent.

"Five of them. Five of us. The numbers work," Jules added in, before Mike almost snapped his neck in two to look round at us.

"He's joking, right? Tell me he's joking, please."

I didn't know whether Mike was aiming his jibe at Diehl, or at Jules, but either way I couldn't really provide him with the answer that he wanted. I raised my eyebrows in what I hoped resembled a shrug, before stepping towards the Germans with the rest of the group.

"I suppose it's my turn to make you look stupid, eh *Michel?*" I jibed, his face crestfallen and stunned.

"We're not actually playing?" he said, jogging to catch up with the rest of us.

The Germans had already removed their tunics, placing them a few yards apart to create a goal on the ground. They chucked two more towards us and Cluzet, as happy as anything, gaily ran to the other end of the courtyard to complete the pitch.

Not one of us took our boiler suits off, nor even tied the top half around our waist, petrified that a German might trip and find one of the plethora of explosives that we had hidden about our person.

I shrugged again towards Mike, "Scared that I'm going to show you up?"

His face burned orange as he berated us all under his breath for being so stupid and happily joining the enemy.

"What choice do we have, Mike?" I whispered once he had finally caught up with me. "They'll think it odd that five Frenchmen don't want to skive off work for at least a few minutes."

He mulled it all over in his mind for a few seconds, his bottom lip disappearing inside his mouth again as he bit down on it, hard. He knew that if he was to leave now, not only would it put the operation in more danger than it already was, he would put the match at risk too.

Diehl laughed and hooted as he realised that he was about to play what was the biggest game of his life. He jogged over to us and tried shaking our hands, but his own were quivering too much to grip hold of us for too long.

"Oh, this is excellent. Simply excellent," he began muttering, switching between his own German tongue and that of the land that he was occupying.

"France against Germany! Again, after so many years!"

"If only he knew who he was really up against," Andrew breathed as he stood alongside me.

"1937 I think you'll find was the last match between these two great nations." He emphasised the 'great' and bowed his head ever so slightly as he did so. "We beat you, of course. Four goals to nil. March it was, in Stuttgart. Of course, I was there. Wouldn't have missed it for anything."

The other soldiers around us began to jog and kick the ball between themselves, while Diehl was still in his own little world in 1937. The rest of my team simply watched him curiously, not preparing themselves for the match in the slightest.

"Stuttgart. Is that where you're from?" I asked, cutting into his daydream.

"Yes…well, just outside. Have you ever been?"

I looked at him and scoffed. Even if he had known that I was an Englishman, the answer would still have been the same.

He shuffled his feet as his face turned a brighter

shade of pink, "No, of course. Sorry."

"Is it a nice place?" I asked, trying to coax him back out of his shell again.

"Stuttgart?" No, not really. But we have the nicest cars, the best in the whole world. Luxury, real fine living."

I caught the sight of Mike peering over Diehl's shoulder, giving a disapproving glare that told me that I should cut off my interaction immediately. I defied the order.

The German continued to talk about Stuttgart, his home, his mother, anything he could think of and some things that he couldn't, tripping and stumbling on his words as he tried earnestly to recall aspects of his life he could no longer remember.

As I listened, I found myself breathless with disbelief. I was an Englishman, in France, talking to a German, about to engage in a game of football. My experience of war could not have been further away from that experienced by the warriors throughout the centuries.

Frustrated that he could not remember the name of the street that he had grown up on, Diehl reached into his tunic. I felt my muscles tighten as I thought a weapon of some description was going to be drawn, but relaxed myself so much when it wasn't, that I almost lost control of my bowels.

He held the small flask up to his lips and knocked his head backwards sharply, letting out a large sigh as the liquid slipped down his neck.

Mike hovered around his side so much, keeping a suspicious eye on the two of us, that he soon found the flask dangling underneath his nostrils.

"You would like some?" Diehl asked, as Mike leant in to sniff it.

"No. I do not drink."

Diehl retracted the flask quickly, in case Mike changed his mind, before wafting it under my nose.

"What about you? Please tell me you don't drink also," he chuckled, his hand tremoring and letting the liquid catch the light of the sunset.

I swallowed hard as I thought about my decision, before taking the flask and lifting it to my lips.

Mike glared at me the entire time I held it in my grasp, as I reasoned with myself that two teetotal factory workers was an irregularity that even a drunk German would have been able to spot.

I felt the liquid burn the tip of my tongue as I pushed it into the flask, to prevent any of the liquid actually passing down my throat.

I coughed gently as I handed it back to him, before I cleared my throat to speak.

"If they catch you with that, you'll be shot."

He chuckled as he took another swig.

"If they catch me sharing it with a Frenchman, I will be shot twice over."

I laughed along with him on that one. He was safe as houses on that charge.

I wasn't French.

22

The game got off to a slow start, with no one really knowing whether we should get going or not. The tentative few kicks of the ball from the Germans eventually grew in their intent, until the light jogging soon turned into hearty sprints, puffing and panting bouncing off the walls on three sides of the pitch.

If only Christopher knew what was going on in here, I thought to myself, as the ball headed my way. He would probably never believe it, but I thought that he would approve of what we were doing. He saw every soldier as a man, no matter what side they were fighting for.

My first few touches of the ball were lacklustre and poor, which I allowed myself, as it had been such a long time since I had last been engaged in such an activity.

I couldn't but help let the smile get the better of me and, no matter how much I tried to suppress it, it kept forcing itself to the surface, until I was puffing away with a big grin on my face.

Despite his reluctance, I could tell that Mike was enjoying it too. He had been a huge football fan and had missed the weekly matches since they had been suspended at the start of the war.

As I lashed the ball from one side of our makeshift pitch to the other, Mike expertly controlling it with the outside of his foot, I almost shouted something at him that would have undoubtedly given the game away.

"Just like Teddy Fenton!" I had almost screamed, Mike's flowing hair reminiscent of the midfielder that had played for his beloved West Ham for the last few seasons.

He looked up at me once he had released the ball towards Jules, with a great big smile on his face.

I did always wonder whether he had the same thought as me in that moment, but I couldn't help but beam back. We were actually enjoying ourselves.

It had been an age since we had been on any kind of sports field together. St John's College, Cambridge was now so far away that it almost seemed like it had never existed, only some weird fixation of my imagination. But mine and Mike's time on the sports grounds in England had most definitely been real.

Mike had, I frequently had to concede, been the better sportsman of the two of us. He took to anything with such a natural ability that it was frustrating, as I spent my hours looking for something that I would somehow be better at.

He had always been in the first teams for everything; the first fifteen for the rugby, first eleven in the cricket, he had even had a brief stint in the lacrosse team. It was a wonder that he had any time left to study at all.

He was a permanent fixture in the first eleven for the football team too, one of the most gifted midfielders that I had ever seen.

I always fancied my chances against him in football though, as my name was always the one that was first on the team sheet, the responsibility of team captain resting solely on my shoulders.

I had always liked the feeling of power that I had over him on the football pitch.

It felt good to be back on the pitch, even if it was a concrete surface and nowhere near the lush fields of England that I had played on before.

There was a sense of freedom that had relinquished me from the grip of war. Just for those few fleeting moments that we played, I felt as though nothing had ever happened, and that we were simply playing one of our fiercest rivals for St John's.

I felt good.

Diehl was still the most vocal one on the pitch, as he jogged around chatting to anyone that would lend half an ear in his direction. I could not tell what it was that he was going on about, even when he was stood right next to me, but before too long he was reluctantly trying to find his feet in the game.

The shouts and grunts were ones that were generally content, and the game carried on in a surprisingly good spirit considering the circumstances. There was a brief moment where Jules landed on his knees with a sickening crack, and I thought for a moment that the German was going to feel the full force of his anger. But, somehow, he managed to bite his tongue.

Diehl suddenly found himself with the ball at his feet and, after a little dallying and debating about what to do with it, he turned, opening his body up towards me.

All I needed now was a pistol, and I would have had a clear shot at his chest with which I was convinced I could bring him down with a quick tap-tap of the trigger.

But, instead, my mind had shifted, from one that was geared up to war, to one that was fixated on the game taking place.

I knew that I would maybe get just the one chance at doing something like this to a German soldier and so, as his chest was wide, the ball trickling around his feet, I knew that I had to get it just right straight away.

There was something about Diehl that I actually quite liked, despite trying my hardest to hate him as I had been taught to do. He seemed as if he was somewhat of a loner, even though he was surrounded by his compatriots on every side.

I felt like, despite the fact I had far more reason to

feel isolated, that I actually felt more at home than he did.

Nevertheless, the opportunity to be able to legitimately clatter into a German soldier, while well behind the lines, was far too good a chance to pass up. He started to jog, picking up speed as he charged down the wing, his head down and staring at the ball.

He barely saw me coming as a result. His body was still wide and opened towards me and as I picked up pace, I questioned whether I was doing the right thing. But, by the time I was able to make any kind of a decision, I was well too late.

I smashed into him and I felt bones strike bones, as my knee painfully smashed into his and we both tumbled to the ground.

Diehl had known of nothing that was coming towards him, and he was still struggling to make sense of what was going on as he crouched on all fours as he tried to get the air back into his lungs.

A few shouts and murmurs grumbled out as I heard even my own teammates agree to a German freekick.

I got back to my feet and dusted down my boiler suit, with a relative ease that I found almost concerning.

"Here," I breathed, offering out my hand to the German, who was scrabbling around on the ground with something. I thought for a moment that I had hit him so hard that one of his eyes had fallen out.

He took my hand and I gripped it hard, before

hauling him up so that he was eye to eye with me once again.

"You..." he looked down towards his hand. "You dropped this."

I let go of his hand as his free palm stretched out towards me.

I found myself staring down into his palm, taking in the sight of the small, modified Clam mine that was meant for operations such as these. It was a small, but powerful device that was made of a magnetic material that allowed it to be planted to anything of value; a railway line, a tank or, in our case, a lathe or boring machine used in factories around the world.

My heart stopped, for longer than it should have done, as I realised what an overwhelming fool I had been. I had neglected to adhere to one of the first things that I had been taught when training for this job.

If you ever had anything of worth in your pockets, you were always meant to make sure that they were secure before embarking on a period of jostling, and I had left the button on my breast pocket undone just minutes before.

I swallowed, hard, as my heart restarted with renewed urgency and I forced the vomit to settle back into the lining of my stomach as I pulled myself together. If I had had the time to take a deep breath, I would have done it, but instead had to make do with a breathless improvisation.

"It's a new fuse for the lathe in machine shop

three. It broke earlier in the day. I was meant to fix it tonight."

I stuffed the explosive into my pocket so hard that there was a danger that the thing would go off there and then, which was what I was hoping for as the seconds ticked by.

Diehl said nothing, but simply carried on staring down at his empty palm, which I noticed now had a large graze on it. I wondered what he was doing, whether he was inspecting his wound or debating whether he should shout at his comrades to tell them what he had seen.

But, as I stared deep into his eyes, he decided against it. There was just a hint of a doubt in his mind, that maybe what he had seen had been his imagination, a result of the concoction that he had been drinking and the exhaustion that dragged his eyes towards the ground.

I sealed my breast pocket and gave it a tug so that it wouldn't make a repeat appearance, but I knew immediately that my effort in the rest of the match would be decidedly lacklustre.

I looked around swiftly and caught sight of Jules staring at the two of us. There was no way that he hadn't seen what had happened, as his eyes were so wide that he found it impossible to blink. Just as he looked as though he was going to burst into tears, I jogged away, picking up the ball from Cluzet before walloping it towards goal.

For a second or two, I was convinced that the only

witness to the incident had been Jules, but as I mulled the incident over in my mind, there was no way that the others had missed it. They had just decided to carry on regardless. It was more dangerous to pretend that something was up.

For the remainder of the match, I took as few touches as possible, instead opting to hit the ball as hard as I could as some form of release. I cared not a jot for the game, or the result, and neither did anyone else on my team for that matter.

My chest was tight and painful for the remainder of the time that we spent out in the courtyard, and I knew already that I had ruined the operation for everyone. We were now too highly strung and besides, we would not have long enough to set the charges now that we had played what seemed like a full ninety minutes with the Germans.

It was only when it became too dark to see where the ball was going, did they concede that it was finally time to return to our duties. We shook hands, some more nervous than others, and parted ways.

No one said anything to me about my little incident, but as I gripped Diehl's hand, he gave me a once over that told me that he knew more than he would care to let on. Everyone knew that he was a drunk, and no one would believe him if he said anything, especially after they had fraternised with the enemy.

I trudged back to the factory, where the others had

gathered, my head down, chin tucked as far into my chest as it would go.

It was Cluzet who eventually suggested that we go our separate ways, the authority in his voice going a long way around the group.

"Try again tomorrow night."

"No. We can't," Andrew blurted. "Tonight is the end of the four weeks. The raids start again tomorrow."

There was a silence for a moment, which Mike took to give me the most murderous of glares.

"It doesn't matter," he said, prying his eyes away from me. "We have to do it tomorrow. We have to try again."

23

Christopher's face was red and blotchy, and it was clear that he had been asleep. The four of us bundling through the door earlier than planned had clearly disturbed him. I couldn't quite believe that one of the biggest operations of my life was meant to be taking place, and the bleary-eyed man in front of me had been making sure that he got all of his beauty sleep.

"What happened? Where's the other chap?"

"Cluzet? He went back home. To his own place," Andrew seemed like the only one capable of speaking.

The rest of us remained silent as Christopher quickly woke up to the fact that it was only just past midnight, and we weren't meant to be out of the factory for another couple of hours at least. And even then, we weren't meant to be stepping inside Jules' home ever again.

None of us wanted to speak, and even Andrew,

who had said only a few words, appeared too exhausted to try and get another syllable out.

My mouth was so dry that my tongue felt as though it had ballooned to the size of another skull inside my own, making it difficult to breathe, never mind speak. A glass of water, that had been sat on the table by the door for however knows long was quickly thrown down my neck, before I went in search of another.

I felt nauseous as I poured from the jug, before launching the liquid down my throat, the moisture doing just enough to alleviate the stress on my lungs.

"What happened? What are you doing here?" Christopher continued, pestering us all for an answer. I probably would have done the same, but in the moment, he irritated me to the point of insanity.

"Oh, that's a fantastic idea. Why don't we all have a pint of the stuff?" he said, sarcastically waving his arms around as the bottle of scotch, hidden under a floorboard, was retrieved and decanted into small glasses.

The bottle was quite quickly reopened and passed around to top us all up. The liquid passed by Christopher, who seemed too flustered to even consider a drink of the stuff.

"Is no one going to tell me what happened?" Christopher exploded, his face puffing red and his eyes bulging.

"Alright!" Mike exploded, so loudly that I caught

the window panes tremor at the murderous tone. "Enough!"

There was a moment of silence, as Mike massaged his forehead, where we all thought that he was about to retell the story, but it seemed as though he just wanted a few seconds of peace.

"What happened?" Christopher repeated, more controlled this time, but just as urgent.

Mike's body stiffened, as he placed the glass rather forcefully down on a side table.

"What happened? What happened?" he began shrieking, as I finally began to fear my accomplice as he flapped and skulked around the room. His voice got higher the more agitated he became, to the point where I became worried that soon no human would be able to make out his tones.

As I just about made out the sorrow and remorse that was quivering behind his agitation, I realised that the guilt that had until now, largely eluded me, was right beside me, as well it should have been.

There was an overwhelming number of emotions suddenly flooding me, from wanting to break down in tears to fighting for myself and pleading my innocence. But I knew all too well that not one of those things would help my predicament in the slightest.

I would simply have to take what was coming to me.

"What happened?!" he squawked again. "What happened indeed!"

"Look Mike, everyone…I—"

Mike shot me a look that sent a bolt of pain straight through my heart. It called me out there and then as someone who had let him down tremendously, but outwardly he said nothing of the sort.

"They wanted a game of football!"

"Who did?"

"The Germans did! Called at us just as we were heading into workshop four! We played with them for over an hour!"

Christopher chewed it over for a second, simply staring at each one of us, in turn, to try and validate the outrageous claims that Mike was making.

"A game of…? But why?"

"They must have been bored," Jules muttered, chewing at a tough piece of bread. "It can't be much fun standing around all day like that."

Christopher's mouth hung open for a moment, processing the time constraints that we had in trying to lay all the explosives before getting out of there. We needed to make sure that every single machine that we wanted to destroy was in fact beyond repair, rather than just taking out the few that we would have managed before the early shift came in at just before four in the morning.

"So," Christopher began, a plan seeming to form in his head, "Is anyone going to tell me what the score was?"

A warped smile appeared on his face, as we all looked up in even more disbelief.

"3-1 to the Germans. We had Jules in goal," Mike said, as Jules shrugged in the corner.

"Sounds like you could have done with an expert winger. Shame I was on the outside really."

"You?" Mike said, laughing a great belly laugh. "Come off it. A winger needs pace and you don't have it, chum."

There was a brief moment where I thought Christopher was offended by the exchange, but he soon saw the funny side. He was warming to Mike and he knew that now was not the time to try and rile him any further.

"So, what's next then?" he asked, confidently taking charge of the situation for the first time since he had arrived in France. "Do we call it off altogether?"

"Absolutely not," Mike blurted, the aggression suddenly returning and putting Christopher back into his place.

"But…the bombers. The time ran out tonight. They could be coming back tomorrow."

It seemed as though the apprehension had got the better of both Andrew and Christopher. They were backing away from the fire, which is not what we needed at all. We needed them right beside us, more fired up and ready to go than they had been tonight.

"We have to try again," Mike started, emotion catching his voice. "We have to. That village can't go through what they've been through again. We've prepared so much. We're ready."

There was a silence that was crying out to be filled.

"Look, if the bombers do come, the chances are they won't hit the factory. They've been trying to hit it for months and all they can do is flatten schools and the police station."

"And what if they do finally hit their target?"

There was another silence, my mind working on overtime as I tried to come up with something reasonable.

"All the better for it. If they do find their target, then it'll mean that all the Germans are somewhere keeping their heads down. Not only that but it'll cover our tracks. They won't even know that we've been there."

No one said a word, there was just the sound of a crusty old piece of bread being tossed and turned inside Jules' mouth. We all sat down in silence, thinking through the impossible situation that we had found ourselves in.

Not only had we just played a football match with the Germans, but we now faced the possibility of trying to blow up a factory at exactly the same time that sixty or seventy bombers were trying to do the exact same thing.

To my surprise, it was Christopher who spoke first.

"Well, we have to do it, don't we? We have no choice but to go again tomorrow night. If the bombers come, let them come."

There was a nodding of heads and a smattering of agreements that went around the room one by one. I felt excited, but there was just one thing that was holding me back; I didn't want to make an even bigger mistake than I had done tonight.

Knocking his drink back in expert fashion, Mike suddenly got up from his chair, slapping his thighs.

"Right, well I'm glad that's sorted. I'm off to bed. With any luck, we won't be getting much sleep tomorrow night."

"You said that last night," Andrew mumbled into his knuckle.

"Yeah, well, unless the Germans want a second leg then I don't think I'll be saying it again."

He chuckled, but quickly cut it short at the thought that a rematch was a very real possibility, especially if they saw the same team back together again.

I let him leave the room, before getting up myself and announcing that I too would be going to get my head down.

Closing the door behind me, I grabbed Mike's shoulder just as he reached the top of the stairs.

"Mike."

"Johnny?"

"Why didn't you tell them…about the, you know. The Clam."

I thought back to what an incompetent fool I had been in leaving my breast pocket open and flapping in the wind.

"Why would I?"

"Because Christopher asked what happened. It happened, didn't it?"

He shrugged, his face pulling itself into an ugly expression that looked as though he had smelled something rotten.

"It would have got me nowhere, Johnny. What would I have gained by getting angry at you for something like that? I could have damn well nearly done the same thing. Besides, it wasn't the reason why we were back here, was it? That's what he really wanted to know."

"Wasn't it? My nerves were shot to bits, I'm sure Jules' were too. I would say it was the whole reason why we lost our bottle tonight."

He continued as if he hadn't heard a word I'd said.

"Look, you didn't tell anyone about my little friend back in *Tours*. So, it's hardly going to be difficult for me to keep that sort of thing from Christopher. What he doesn't know won't hurt him."

"What happened with you and that girl in *Tours* was completely different, Mike."

His face fell as he thought back to our time in *Tours*, as did my own mind, and how much I had started to miss Suzanne. She had barely featured in my thoughts for days, which was probably a good thing. She was too much of a distraction.

"It wasn't any different Johnny. Both were mistakes. Both could have got us killed."

He stared at me for a moment, his deep, set-back eye sockets disappearing in the darkness as we shared a moment of peace, just the two of us, for the first time in months. This was how I had pictured it all, just the two of us, against the whole of the German army. No one else to get in our way or to distract our thoughts.

He snorted, before his lips widened to reveal his warm smile. I couldn't help but follow his example and, within seconds, we were sharing a hearty laughter that had to be suppressed, for fear of waking little Georges up.

"Keep your chin up, Johnny. This war won't go on forever."

"I should hope not."

He slapped me on the arm, "Good night, old fruit."

"Good night, Mike."

I turned away from him, feeling readier than ever to get my head down onto a pillow and sleep. My mind was abuzz with the thoughts of the evening, as well as the excitement and enthusiasm of wanting the day to pass me by quickly.

The feeling of fire in my belly was slowly being stoked, and I could feel the desire to get my teeth stuck into the Germans once more.

I readied myself for bed, as best I could. But, as I pressed my head into the pillow, Mike's snores already echoing down the hallway, my mind was filled with a thousand and one other things that were preventing me from sleeping.

Never mind, I thought to myself, at least it would keep the nightmares at bay.

24

So far, so good.

I knew I shouldn't have thought it the second that it came to my mind, but I was sure that I hadn't been the only one to allow the confidence to enter my consciousness.

Getting past the sentries had been the easy part, Diehl had been on duty and, apart from one or two remarks about the football match, we had passed through without any hindrances.

We were lighter too as, apart from our pistols and revolvers, we had no weapons on us whatsoever. It had been far easier to dump them in the factory and retrieve them later on.

A few men still milled around in the factory, paying next to no attention to us whatsoever. Despite the Germans taking over his factory, Peintre's pockets were still deeper than mine ever would be, and Cluzet had managed to persuade him to slide a few notes the way of those who were working that night.

I didn't know how they were going to avoid being in the workshops when the explosives went off, but all I could hope for was that they managed to get out and stay out.

The cupboard, from what I could see, was stuffed to the rafters with everything that someone might need to scrub down a factory floor to within an inch of its life. There were several mops, with accompanying buckets, as well as filthened rags that had clearly been used to wipe down some of the machines. A strong stench wafted from the cupboard, a sickly smell that tried to mask the filth with an inadequate scent of freshness, but I couldn't quite tell if the smell was from the cupboard, or from Cluzet.

Cluzet leant into the cupboard, his boiler suit tied around his waist and his shirt untucked, to reach in and bring out our toys like Aladdin's cave. His trousers slipped as he grunted, his buttocks coming on show, giving rise to a simultaneous groan as we all turned our faces away.

"Oh, come on Cluzet. Your face was ugly enough."

"Sorry," he grunted, sniffing loudly but doing nothing to sort out his falling clothing.

It wasn't a pretty sight, and the situation considerably worsened as he leant further and further into the cupboard, retrieving things from the depths of darkness.

"Take these then, come on. Come on."

He grunted impatiently, passing two jute bags over his head and to the nearest man behind him.

Jules grabbed them, inspecting them.

"Cluzet, this bag is full of rags…this one old bolts and things."

"Ah, right. Those must have been hiding the explosives. I'm sure they're in here somewhere."

I stepped away from the group, moving to one of the machines and running my hand over a piece of pre-fabricated steel. It was cool and smooth, and I marvelled at the way something so basic and calming could soon be turned into a weapon of war.

I turned and looked at the backs of the four other men that I was with. Pushing my hand into my pocket, I pulled the pistol into my palm, as I stared towards the door.

As we had stood there, all waiting for Cluzet to produce the weapons, I had grown increasingly paranoid that we had been found out. The Germans had found the explosives, moved them, and were now poised for the strike that caught the men in the act of retrieving them.

As selfish as it was, I was hoping that by being away from them, I could pass myself off as just another worker. Failing that, I could raise the alarm by firing a few rounds through my pocket.

"Cluzet man, you haven't even bothered to hide them," Mike hissed, so loudly that some of the other employees turned their heads to the noise.

"I didn't need to," the Frenchman replied. "The Germans never come in here anyway."

"But some of your lot do. How do you know you can trust all of them?"

"When your country is occupied, you'll know how it feels. They're all on our side."

"Has he never heard of fifth columnists?" Mike breathed to me as he left the group also. I could feel the anger seeping out of him, the heat exuding from his reddened skin like a boiler. I snorted softly as he walked past, but I was worried about him.

A degree of anxiety and nerves was expected, in fact it was actively encouraged, it was what would keep us on our toes and consequently, alive. But Mike was allowing his nerves to manifest as impatience, frustration. That sort of thing would get him killed.

But it was a thought that I would rather have not entertained, and so I pushed it away by amusing myself with other things.

My feet were silent as I moved around the workshop, relocating tools and admiring pieces of pre-production, which I was sure would end up frustrating the other workers no end. But, if everything went well, in a few hours this workshop would be nothing more than a dusty bowl of rubble.

Bags were being fumbled from the cupboard now, with Cluzet practically naked as he refused to pull his boiler suit back up. The bags were visibly heavier than the few before, and so I was confident that the Germans had not simply replaced our explosives with sponges and other cleaning equipment. We were back on track.

The faces that had spoken of annoyance and paranoia slowly eased, and my confidence in each of them grew once again to levels that spoke of a degree of comfort.

Mike and Andrew were the two that I felt I could trust the most; they had, after all, received extensive training in how to rig up machines for demolition. Jules would come in close behind, receiving only a minimal amount of theoretical training in what to do. Cluzet on the other hand worried me greatly.

It was why Mike, Andrew and I had been given charge of the more important machines, in workshop one, three and four. That was where most of the production was done. The other two had slightly less important aims; to destroy the two assembly workshops.

They weren't essential targets, but the more damage we could do, the more of the German's pride we could dent.

Above all the others though, the one who made my heart flutter with an overwhelming anxiety was the man who had the least responsibility, but the one who could effectively end it all for us; Christopher.

He was back at the safe house, after seating himself in the very same café an hour or two before as we attempted entry into the factory again. After watching us in, it would be his job to return back to Jules' home, and begin discarding anything and everything that could have possibly tied us to the area.

The blueprints that Peintre had supplied us with would have been thrown into the fire, along with any other documents that could have led back to us.

Slowly, I would find myself stripped of everything that I had; my possessions, my safe haven, my identity. If Christopher managed to do everything correctly, then I, along with Mike and Andrew, would become a grey man.

I would soon find myself with nothing, nothing to be proud of or show for. I had been in that position before, but I could not stop my mind from wandering to the thoughts of one night in particular that had stood out over all the others.

In the space of a single second, I had gone from having possessions, a home, a family, to nothing at all apart from a couple of cold corpses and a pile of smoking rubble. It had stolen everything that I had, including my sanity. It was why I had to make sure that we saw the factory destroyed.

Georges had been through the same thing as me, seeing his mother blown to pieces in much the same way that I had seen my wife. It had happened a hundred times over, right the way across the continent, and if I could stop it happening to a single other person, then I would go above and beyond to do it.

As if the world around me had been reading my thoughts, there was a sudden growl, low and consistent, a moan that I had heard a hundred times before.

The air raid siren continued to sound, as the panicked faces all around us suddenly became even more alarmed, none more so than Cluzet, who appeared to lose hope completely.

My thoughts more or less immediately turned to the boys who were in the air, the bombers full to bursting with bombs wriggling to fall from their bays.

I wondered about who was up there and whether they were as nervous as I was. I prayed to anyone that would listen that they hadn't used their time off to do some target practice, and that no new device had been invented in the interim to make their bombs fall directly on our heads.

I had always felt so free and unrestricted when I was up in the air, but as I thought of the others who were slowly gaining on me, I had never felt so tied up and conflicted in all my life.

"We need this! Cover!" shouted Andrew, his voice full of hope and optimism, his face betraying his true emotions.

It was no stain on his character, as every face that stood there was one of absolute horror and terror, as everyone silently passed the baton of leadership to the next man.

"What now?" shouted Jules, the sirens and clamour from outside enough to make any man go deaf.

"We carry on as normal!" Mike replied, taking some of the Clams from the bag and stuffing them in his pockets, along with some plastic explosive.

"Wait!" Cluzet called, as he buried his hand in another bag and, for a moment, I thought he had discovered something in the bag that would change our lives forever. "We wait here. For a few minutes. Let the Germans man their posts and get to shelter. Then we'll have free roam over the whole factory. They'll be looking to the skies."

We stood around in expectation for a minute or two, slowly taking our explosives and tucking them away in our pockets. I took one Clam and placed it in my breast pocket, making sure that the button was securely fastened, giving it a soft tug. Mike caught my eye and smiled wryly.

"Everyone clear on what they are doing?" I called; the men huddled around me deafened by my shouts. "Go over it again?" I suggested, lowering my tone so that I did not needlessly fill the now-empty hall.

One by one the men around me spoke, relaying the instructions that I had heard a thousand times already. It never did any harm to make sure that we were all singing from the same hymn sheet, especially when explosives were involved, men had lost fingers and sometimes more by not knowing what the plan was.

It got to my turn and, for a second, I froze, as I struggled to recall what it was I was doing. An elbow to the ribs from Mike quickly brought me back into the room.

"Workshop four. The two lathes, boring machine and that weird profiling machine that Cluzet loves so much. Then to clear out the workshop office of any documents."

Cluzet went to defend his love of the profiling machine, but ultimately decided against it, leaving a silence to fill the void where men's voices had been a moment ago.

The lack of noise was horrifying, as the sound of the sirens slowly gave up, and my ears strained to make out any noise at all.

"Well, good luck then. See you on the other side," Andrew muttered, shaking hands with each of us. We all did likewise, wishing each other well and wondering what the 'other side' actually meant.

The sound of soft footsteps departing in their plimsolls was slowly trumped by a more ominous, sobering and alarming sound. There was a drone of bombers looming over us, four-engined ones. There was no doubt about that.

25

I stood still for a moment. I looked around me, my mind slowly filtering out all the noise of the outside world until there was nothing left but my breathing and the sound of blood pumping through my veins.

The cold, damp concrete walls stared back at me, the whole workshop void of any movement whatsoever, a stark contrast to how it had been just a few hours before in daylight.

Tools had been laid down at a moment's notice, and nothing that belonged to anyone, apart from a few old boiler suits hung up at the far end, seemed to remain in the room.

As I looked around, visualising all of my movements before I even actioned them, I felt powerful, as if the whole workshop was my own. In that moment, as the unforgiving drone of bombers drew closer and closer, I strangely felt in control. I had not often felt like that since being in this war. My fate had almost always been in the hands of someone else.

I had several options before me. One was to do the job that I had been sent there to do, the other was one that at best amounted to cowardice, at worst leaving my friends in the lurch.

I couldn't abandon my efforts now, not after everything I had seen and done in the run-up. I had to thaw my feet out and get moving and forget the glaringly obvious chance of death as the bombers roared ever closer.

The floor was damp, and a few puddles still lingered, where the various machines had been cooled or the steel was needed urgently to be transported elsewhere. My feet sploshed in them as I padded across the workshop, but otherwise, the soles of my plimsoles, although impossibly thin, did a good job of keeping my movements as silent as possible.

I felt as though I was back in the cockpit of my Hurricane, strapped in and preparing to face the Germans down with nothing but a couple of canons and a silk parachute strapped to my back. That was the last time that I had felt properly in control, and not at the mercy of someone else.

If I was shot down by a Messerschmitt, it wasn't because the other pilot had been better than me or his aircraft more advanced, but it was because I had messed up. I had flown too straight and level for too long, or had not been attentive enough to notice his advance.

It was the same as I drew up close to the first machine, its large drill hanging perilously over an untouched sheet of metal, ready to pierce holes into it as the operator demanded.

The concrete walls around me began to shake and shout, as the bellowing engines grew closer and the anti-aircraft guns suddenly began to open up in response. The German pom-pom guns sounded very different to the British ones, and it was something that I had struggled to get used to ever since being in France. They were louder, deeper, as if they were more mature and were far more serious in attempting to shoot something down.

It was likely to be the case, as I had always thought that our own pom-poms were nothing more than an attempt to reassure the people who were subjected to the bombing. I had never heard a first-hand account of a result. It had always come from a friend of a friend.

A sudden urgency rushed to my mind, my hands instantly perspiring, and the drum beat of my heart resounding just in time to hear the first few bombs landing a mile or two away. I began counting the seconds between each rapid burst of ack-ack fire, like I did as a child to work out how far away the thunder was.

It was a nothing exercise, I knew that, but it made me feel calmer somehow, and allowed the pulsating blood to settle slightly and clear my mind.

I wiped the sweat from my brow, in turn pressing

my hands down the sides of my boiler suit, to rid myself of the perspiration and grease that was building up all around me. I exhaled sharply as I forced myself to get to work.

I had already wasted five minutes. The others would have been able to set at least one charge up by now.

I felt sick as I began to pull my tools from my pockets. I was confident that this was the best thing to do, and if I was to end up killing someone as a result of my sabotage then it was far better than an entire village being slowly wiped out.

But there was still something that was making my hands quake. Something in the back of my mind.

I tossed the Clam around in my palms for a few moments, letting its weight drag my arms down momentarily before I remembered that this wasn't a child's toy. It was sent to us for a purpose, one that I was doing nothing to help fulfil.

Filled with visions of Georges crying over the corpse of his mother, I knelt down behind the boring machine, finding the motor and allowing the Clam's magnets to snap itself to the metal. It was in a good position, in the hope that it would take out as many of the internal components as was possible from such a small blast.

I set the fuse, allowing the acid to begin burning through a thin piece of metal, that would hopefully set the whole charge off after sixty minutes. The second that I had set that charge off and ticking, it was as if a bolt of electricity had been pumped into my limbs. My fingers began to work quicker than they ever had done before, my mind in overdrive and darting everywhere to keep watch while I worked.

I moved from one machine to the next, ticking them off mentally one by one as I approved of my own handiwork.

Kneeling down behind the final machine, I slipped the Clam into place and allowed the fuse to start doing its thing. I pulled the last thing that was in my little bag, in a similar routine to the other machines.

The explosive in my hand was tense but malleable, like a piece of clay that had been refrigerated. It was an odd green colour, like the pigment had been washed out, but a faint hint of it remained. I wished that the same could have been said for the stench that it gave off, but the sweet, nutty smell that wafted its way to my nostrils had already taken the claim for the pounding skull ache that I now possessed.

The advice was to make sure the Explosive 808 was in contact with your skin for as short a time as possible and, until now, it had never stayed in physical contact with my skin for anything longer than ten seconds.

As I worked on the last machine, my hands began to itch terribly, and I could not work out if it was the paranoia or a genuine complaint that was causing them to do so.

My whole body flinched as a bomb detonated somewhere outside the walls of the factory, followed by a whole series more, and I watched as the window panes that ran along the top perimeter of the workshop flexed, and thought about shattering into tiny pieces.

They didn't and, as the first wave of bombers roared overhead, I knew that I had to get a move on. The second would not be all that far behind.

I moulded the plastic explosive in a 'U' shape position, directly underneath the clam, so that it was almost touching it. The plastic explosive was powerful, but not quite powerful enough to cripple the workshop.

The 808 was there just as a backup. We needed to be certain that none of the machines were operable, and so, just to make sure, we were using the plastic explosive as a fail-safe. Those Clams would be detonating, one way or another.

I pushed two time-pencil fuses into the plastic carefully. I knew that no amount of force would make the 808 detonate, but I was always as careful as I could be. There was no point in taking risks.

I stepped back from my handiwork and inspected the plastic explosive, the two white tips of the pencils proudly sticking out just enough so that I could pull the starting pin, which would start the process of the pencil slowly stretching a piece of thin metal. Once that snapped, the whole charge would go up, taking the Clam, and the machine, with it.

But I was hoping that the plastic would not be needed, placing my faith in the fuses that were inserted into the Clams.

I checked my watch. I had been in there twenty minutes. Fifteen minutes or so since the first fuse had begun to get to work.

I suddenly got very itchy feet.

The timers on the clams were set to sixty minutes. The L-Delay pencils were set to two hours. But none of them were well-known for their reliability to keep to their schedules.

Some of them had been known to go off half an hour before they were supposed to. Which gave me fifteen minutes to get well clear.

I knelt back behind the machine and gathered up a few of the bits and pieces that I had not used. The L-Delays were hard to come by and useful, and so I wanted to make sure that I still had all the spares on my possession before I left the workshop.

Suddenly, above all the noise of the continuing air raid, I heard something. It was a noise like nothing I had heard for quite some time, and I had become so wrapped up in prepping the machines for demolition, that I had almost forgotten what it sounded like.

There was a human cough, followed by some rather laboured and struggling breathing.

I froze. My mind raced.

I made sure that my entire body was hidden behind the machine, my eyes glaring at the whacking great explosive charge that I had set on it not two minutes ago.

I knew it couldn't have been one of the others. That hadn't been part of the plan. The first and only person to go into the workshops was the saboteur of each room.

I was fairly confident too that it wouldn't have been one of the other workers. They had been paid to stay out of our way and now it seemed like the entire RAF was bearing down on *Besançon,* I couldn't imagine any one of them wanting to stay above ground any longer than they needed to.

I peered between the machine, trying to see in the poor light what the source of the sound had been.

Whoever it was, he seemed totally oblivious to the air raid that was raging all around him, as my body grimaced and flinched as another volley of ack-ack could be felt from a matter of yards away.

He continued to stand in the doorway, his shoulders back and chest puffed out, quite like he would have been had he been out on parade. But the rest of him told me that he could not have been further away from a parade; his tunic was half tucked in and half out, a button here or there clearly not together and his rifle precariously sliding off his shoulder.

He swayed softly as he began rummaging through the pockets of the few boiler suits that were hung up by the door.

He was stealing from them.

He saw something he liked the look of, let out a

low whistle before stashing it away in his inside pocket.

Briskly, he spun around, and I caught my chin on the side of the machine as I flopped to the floor to keep myself concealed.

He began muttering to himself, concentrated and focused, before the sound of his boots disturbing the puddles began to vibrate through the workshop. He was getting closer, still muttering something that I could not quite work out.

His feet stopped. So did the muttering. I risked looking around the side of the machine. He was no more than ten yards away from me now. And what I could see made me almost lose control of every emotion in my body.

He had seen the Clams. He had seen the 808. The daft beggar was inspecting them all, one by one.

It simply had to be the most unfortunate night of my life.

26

I couldn't help but kick myself, for what I was not sure, as I did not think I had done all that much wrong. But what I did know was that the German was still taking his time to inspect the charge on the machine, and that if I gave him much more time, then he would not hesitate to tell all his chums outside what was going on.

In short, I knew that I had to act.

I held my breath as I heard the figure shuffling about, his boots grinding on the concrete floor as he began to turn around and walk in a different direction. His footsteps were calm and controlled, not the rapid and sharp ones that I had been expecting.

Nor were they running for the door at the far end of the workshop. They were advancing further into the room. He hadn't believed what he had seen. He was going to need to check all the other machines first.

My skull felt as though it was about to explode as he stopped just on the other side of the machine that I was crouched behind. My knees creaked and threatened to seize up right when I needed them.

He was so close that I could almost feel the warmth of his breath as he muttered, the sound of his nail against the cold steel scraping through my head.

My word, he wanted to be absolutely certain.

I felt his legs straighten, as he exhaled slowly, as if he knew that this day had only been around the corner. As he took one step back, his boot landing in another puddle, I could imagine him, just a yard or two away, accepting defeat.

I couldn't though. I had to do something. Finally, the figure gave me my chance.

He turned on the concrete, sliding more than anything through the puddle as he rotated on his heel.

I sprung up, my knees moaning in agony but nonetheless compliant. I lunged at the figure, as fast as I could. But it wasn't quite quick enough.

The figure had just enough time to turn, his unkempt shirt tails and belt flashing me as he did so.

I got a good look at him for half a second or so and immediately felt quite stupid. But it was all too late.

I should have known by the way that he was dressed. I should have been able to see by the way that he held himself, or perhaps the biggest giveaway, the way that he had swayed.

I was now face to face with Diehl.

If only I had known, then there might have been a chance of getting to him before he saw the charges and try to pass the whole affair off as being in hiding from the bombs. If I had just managed to get to him earlier, then I might have simply been able to engage him in some chat and a cigarette, and he wouldn't have been any the wiser.

But I had hidden myself, restricting my vision and clouding my judgement. I had made an error, and now it was too late to rectify it.

My fist carved through the air bullishly as it connected with Diehl's face. A shooting pain erupted over my knuckle, and I felt my thumb give way under the pressure. Ignoring my own pain, I focused on Diehl's, as his face seemed to crumple like an accordion, but somehow, he managed to stay standing.

Diehl seemed to wait for a moment or two before doing anything, as if he had been betrayed by his own mother and couldn't quite believe it. I knew that he was slow, but the time between being struck and the eventual stagger backwards was quite something.

His feet splashed in the puddles noisily, as my silent footwork advanced towards him, closing the gap.

It wasn't enough to prevent him from being able to catch his falling rifle though and, levelling it towards me, there was a horrifying moment where I was able to look into the black tunnel of the barrel and make a peace with myself.

I flinched as I felt, rather than saw, a round eject

from his rifle, the air popping as it punched through the air just above my head.

The gunshot had echoed so fantastically off the walls that I was almost completely deaf immediately after, but somehow, I still managed to make out the round pinging off one of the smaller profiling machines left at the side of the workshop.

All my muscles suddenly relaxed, as if relieved that they were not required to absorb a rifle round.

My blood suddenly began to surge, and I felt all the veins in my arms suddenly bulge as I turned my knuckles white by balling them into tight fists. A bruise had already developed on my right hand, of that I was quite sure, the purples and blues already so radiant that I could see them out of the corner of my eye.

I couldn't focus on anything else however, apart from the man in front of me who was struggling ineptly with the bolt of his rifle. It was as if a child was operating it, the weakness of his fingers and the apparent lack of dexterity making it near enough impossible for him to both grip the bolt and pull it back towards him.

It was the kind of situation that I almost found laughable and, briefly, the thought of helping him out almost crossed my mind.

But I knew that he simply could not get another round off. If he did then he risked alerting the entire German presence at the factory to the situation but, perhaps selfishly, he risked sending the entire workshop up in one giant fireball, myself included.

It was not the kind of dignified, heroic end that I had planned for myself, instead wanting to go as a valiant king in battle, in front of his men, rather than at the hands of an inebriated, immoral enemy who could barely tie his own shoelaces.

In an ideal world I would have had time to reach for my weapon, to find a piece of steel that I could use to hit him with or attempt another punch. But I didn't have time for any of them, and there was no guarantee that I would still be able to bring him to the floor with those either.

Instead, I did all that I thought I could do. I stepped forward aggressively, springing from the floor and collided into him with an almighty thump. We were able to lock eyes while we both collapsed to the ground, in a momentary freefall in which neither of us could really do anything to the other. We just waited.

His head cracked back into the concrete floor; the sickening snap just as painful for me as it was for him. Neither of us could breathe for a second or two, but both of us knew that the fight had to continue.

My forearm had come to rest on his throat, so immediately I began to apply all the pressure that I could onto it, his eyes bulging the further down I was able to press. My aim was to force my forearm all the way into the ground, and I used my entire bodyweight to press down, my face only an inch away from his as I snarled.

It wasn't out of a laborious output that I growled, but it was something that I had been taught to do.

"Do anything to get the upper hand. Bark if you have to. If it makes it sound like you're hell-bent on killing the man, do it."

I continued to curl my lips and let out an aggressive moan, but it seemed to have the opposite effect on Diehl. His legs suddenly grew in strength as he bucked and kicked, his mouth opening and closing like a fish out of water.

It was only then that I realised he was making one final, overwhelming, last stand to stay alive. The stars would be twinkling in his eyes now, the headache threatening to burst out of his skull.

This was when he was at his most dangerous. I pressed down further, forcing my body closer to the ground.

There was a sudden fire in my face, and I had no option but to let up on some of the pressure that I had applied to Diehl's neck. But I couldn't recoil in the way that I had wanted to, especially after Diehl sank his teeth further into my cheek.

At first, I felt the skin simply pierce, but within seconds blood was pouring out of the wound and into Diehl's mouth, as he spat the warm mixture back out onto me as he tried to stop himself from drowning.

I transferred all my power and effort away from my forearm, yanking my head backwards in a move I knew would only serve to spite me. I left a good chunk of my cheek in Diehl's mouth, as the flesh ripped as easily as a sheet of the steel in the very same workshop.

I let out a howl, not too dissimilar from my murderous growl, but noticeably without the killer instinct that I thought I had possessed.

The stars had obviously affected Diehl more than I had realised, as he waved his hands about flamboyantly, temporarily blinded, before he tried to grip hold of my face and simultaneously drag me in closer to him.

The pain quickly took hold in my face but, although I could feel it nicely, it was barely registering in my thoughts. It was the last thing that I was going to worry about.

I had become so focused on Diehl's face, blood dripping from his canines like a wolf, that I could have had an entire garrison of German troops in the same room, all pointing their weapons in my direction, and I would have been none the wiser.

I wasn't even entirely sure if the air raid was still continuing, everything in my world seemed so silent.

Diehl's left hand was gripped onto the top of my boiler suit, and he was trying to drag me in towards him, his right arm flailed out to the side and motionless. I reasoned that perhaps it was broken or dislocated in some way.

I pulled backwards from him, raising my fist high above my head and bringing it down on his face once again like a whack-a-mole. Blood spurted out from every possible orifice and there was now so much all over his face that I could not distinguish between which was mine and what was his.

I repeated my motions, as teeth started to disappear from inside Diehl's mouth.

At least he won't be biting me again, any time soon.

It was only as I raised my fist for the third time that I realised that I had made a grave error in my judgement. Diehl's right arm hadn't been dislocated or broken. It hadn't even been motionless as I had thought.

It had been brushing the ground searching for something. Something that Diehl knew was right near him.

The first that I knew about it was the feeling of the solid wooden receiver connecting with the side of my skull, just above my cheekbone in the area that always felt softest.

I fell sideways onto the ground, soothing myself in a puddle of cold water for nothing more than a moment.

Only adrenaline was keeping me going now, as I felt my body beginning to falter, and show the first few signs of wanting to give up.

The stars, that had blinded Diehl a few seconds ago, were now blighting me and, as I rolled, I could not distinguish any of the faint outlines that I could see.

I based all my next movements on the light that I could just about make out.

A large, looming darkness suddenly encompassed my entire vision.

Rolling to one side, I thrust my hand in my trouser pocket, gripping the tiny pistol that I had stowed away. I hadn't wanted to use it, for fear of making too much noise, but that ship had already sailed.

With no time to draw it out from my pocket, I simply levelled it towards the shadow that was coming down on me and squeezed the trigger as many times as my battered fingers would allow.

All in all, I think five or six rounds must have been ejected. I did not know how many had actually entered Diehl's body. All I could tell was that at least some of them must have.

Diehl flopped to the floor, his rifle landing with a clatter and with one arm resting over my own.

There was no movement from him. I couldn't even hear him breathing.

Fully aware that I did not have an abundance of time at my disposal, I painfully heaved myself onto my knees, and vomited onto the ground.

The stars were still bursting in my eyes as I woozily got to my feet.

27

There seemed to be a ripple effect as the sounds that had echoed slowly bounced off the walls one by one, reaching my ears but struggling to make themselves known. I strained for a moment or two to try and hear something else, holding my breath and earnestly hoping to hear a noise that would fill me with hope, rather than dread.

But, as I knew full well, nothing came. No one was coming to my rescue. My fate lay solely in my hands and mine alone.

I looked at them for a second, palms facing the sky as if in some kind of prayer. They were soaked in blood, with skin hanging off the heel of my hand as it had grazed along the floor. The only pain that I felt was as I looked at them, the searing agony in my skull taking over the second that I looked away.

It was odd though, as I debated which pain I would rather focus on for a prolonged period of time, my knuckles a bubbling blue and beginning to swell, that I did not feel all that tired. I was in more pain than I had ever been in my life previous, and yet I still felt fired up enough that another Diehl could come stumbling through the door, and I would feel ready for another fight instantly.

It was probably just as well, as the ruckus that we had caused would more than likely have alerted at least one person to the proceedings of workshop four and, depending on how much they valued Diehl's life, they would be making their way towards me rather soon.

I began to stagger, my legs a wobbling mess despite the fact that they had perhaps come off better than any other part of my body. I was fighting the desire to turn around, stumble to each of the machines one by one, to make sure that Diehl had not been able to fiddle with any of the charges and disable any of them.

But I knew that I was running out of time. Even if the Germans weren't on their way, the bomber boys were, and the sounds of falling bombs was tripping tantalisingly close.

With a huge sigh, I pushed myself off one of the machines, confident enough that Diehl possessed neither the know-how nor the presence of mind to have gone about deactivating all of the Clams, in the short space of time that he had been inspecting them.

In one, final act of defiance, Diehl made it excruciatingly difficult for me to be able to move his body, as the last few gasps of air that still lingered ineffectually in his lungs, passed over his vocal cords to allow his final moan of life.

His eyes were set half-open, in a stare that looked straight through everything, seeing plenty, but unable to register a thing.

Pulling his arms high above his head, his rapidly-cooling body was tugged just under the nearest rigged machine, as I struggled to prop him up against it. By the time that I had finished, his head was a matter of inches away from the very explosive that he had seemed so keen to investigate.

There was an element of sadness that hovered in the back of my throat as I positioned him there, as it was only innate human curiosity that had ended up killing him. Now, all being well, his body would be long gone, along with the explosions that he would have ultimately tried to prevent.

I would have done exactly the same thing as him. We weren't really all that different.

With little time to recover, I began searching around in my pocket for the pistol, which was still a little lukewarm from suddenly being called into action.

My eyes were marginally better, but I still struggled to feed the new ammunition into the magazine of the pistol, as the stars continued to burst in my direct line of sight. Fortunately, I had fed small rounds into the magazine so many times that I could do it with my eyes closed, which was what I ultimately found myself doing.

Leaning against one of the production tables, I felt around until I found a rag, oily and greasy after many hours of wiping down the profiling machine. Brushing it against my face made the gaping wound in my cheek burn intensely, and I could feel loose bits of skin hanging carelessly and stubbornly refusing to let go.

Wincing, I did all that I could to try and get rid of as much blood as possible, and it even helped ever so slightly with the stars that were still twinkling.

The pain was beginning to set in. It was no longer just in my skin or on the tips of my fingers, but it was being pumped around me, as if my blood was toxic and was infecting every part of me. Even my bones were beginning to bruise and scream with pain.

I needed to move. Run it off had always been the mantra of every player in the St John's first eleven football team. I would need a bit of that spirit now to get me through.

As I reached the door of the workshop, there was one last cursory sweep of the room that would soon be nothing more than rubble. A final resting place for Diehl.

I could make out little, but it gave me the satisfaction of a job well done nevertheless, despite the fact that there was almost certainly another few hours before I could relax.

I felt my way through the corridors, as my eyes

continued to struggle with the one purpose for which they were there.

It helped tremendously that I had been here before, and had paid close attention to every minute detail, every nail that stuck from the wall, every light switch that marked a few paces closer to my end goal.

I had spent hours poring over the plans that Peintre had given to us and felt like I knew the factory better than the man who had worked there for thirty-odd years. I moved quickly, with purpose and determination, which was surprising considering my energy was dropping significantly with every pace that I managed to muster, each one taking me by surprise now.

The ringing in my ears slowly began to subside, although the headache that it had induced remained with no sign of wanting to leave. But what filled the void that had once been a numbing ring, left me with such a dread that I longed for the deafness to return.

The air raid was continuing to thump on overhead, and I supposed we must have been on the third wave of bombers by now. I guessed that the bomber boys had been stockpiling much of their ordnance for a month and were now unleashing pure fury in order to never have to fly here again.

I could make out the sound of shattered glass twinkling to the floor as I passed by offices and smaller workshops, as the glass that had flexed so defiantly was finally giving way.

The bombs too were adding to the cacophony of

noise, as for the first time they began to connect with the walls of the factory, shaking the ground with such a force that I expected it to open up at a moment's notice.

I stopped. I had felt the last row of switches. Two side by side with another slightly below the first.

Reaching out blindly to my left, I gripped the door handle. It was chilled and quite refreshing to my sweaty and bruised hands, but I could not bring myself to turn it.

I needed to prepare myself.

Faintly, somewhere in the background, I could make out the soft crackle and pop of a fire that had started up some way down the corridor. I hoped that it was contained, for now, but, owing to the possibility that the bomber boys had dropped incendiaries in order to guide the others to the target, I had to assume that it wasn't.

Up until that moment, I had been in the relative safety of the factory. I knew my way around, even if half-blind. But, outside the door was a world of fury and hatred, and not just from the Germans. As soon as I stepped outside, I would be more susceptible to the debris and destruction that surfed around in the night sky.

I exhaled. My eyes were still no better, but I knew I could not risk staying inside a second longer, I could already feel the heat beginning to gently warm my clammy skin.

I yanked at the handle sharply and flung it open,

taking half a second to allow the icy cold stream of midnight air to pummel me in the face. The noise ratcheted up ten notches as I stood there, as the purer sound of aircraft engines was infused with the sound of fires and running water.

Men shouted from all directions as they poured whatever they could on the inferno that was heating the entire town. The bomber boys had already made a big mess.

I knew that I was in an alleyway, that ran down the side of the factory and towards the two large generators that Cluzet had shown us previously.

But I wasn't expecting any movement.

Sensing something in front of me, a man an inch or two shorter, I pulled the pistol up in front of me. I braced myself.

I squeezed the trigger, the pads of my fingers bulging as I applied the pressure. The figure said nothing in the short second or two that it had taken me to level the weapon towards him and apply a force to the curved steel of the trigger.

But then, a grunt. One that I could recognise.

"Jean?"

Instantly, the pistol slipped from my grip and clattered to the floor, me along with it, as I realised that the voice belonged to none other than the man who had been alongside me for so many years; Mike.

I tried to say his name, but nothing would grumble from my mouth.

I felt several other pairs of hands grip me under my arms and heave me back to my feet.

"Come on, we had better get you out of here."

I stumbled as the two men either side of me tried to take some weight off my feet. It had only been a handful of seconds, but I had already started to feel the benefits of being able to relax.

"Did everyone get on alright? All the Clams were set?"

"Yes, they got on a lot better than you," Mike returned, as my vision got less hazy and I could make out his pistol-wielding hand, as it led our advance through the alleyway.

"It was Diehl," I said, letting out a low moan as one of the men inadvertently brushed my cheek.

"Diehl?" Mike said, chuckling sadistically. "Blimey, if that's what a drunk German is able to do to you, I'd hate to see what a sober one will do."

"Shut up. I got all my charges set. That was the job, wasn't it?"

"Yes. But that was meant to be the easy bit!" I could make out his toothy smile looking back at me, with which I could only return with a bloody grin. I was in pain, but I felt on top of the world.

"Can you walk?"

"Yes," I mumbled, as Andrew and Jules set me down on top of a pile of discarded equipment.

"Good, because you're on your own after this bit."

"Fine. I'm okay."

There was a momentary pause, in which a huge

eruption suddenly bawled from the direction of the front of the factory.

"Christopher's going to be mad if that was his café," Andrew quipped, a ripple of laughter half-heartedly forcing itself out into the air. "I guess we should say goodbye."

"Yes, and make it quick," Mike said, as a series of handshakes were exchanged, while Cluzet set the final few charges on the imposing generators.

"Cluzet," Mike said, holding out his hand. "Don't go home, my friend. Find somewhere safe to hide. Just don't go home."

Cluzet chuckled, wiped his hand down his boiler suit and took Mike's hand.

"My friend, I have nowhere else to go."

28

The incandescent rage of the air raid continued to swell all around me, as if a sleeping giant had been sedentary for thousands of years and had finally been prodded into action. I had never heard a cacophony of destruction and pain quite like it.

There was a rawness to it, one that struck me through the heart with a piercing arrow, at the thought that people were dying all around me, good people, when if we had succeeded the first time around, none of this would have been happening.

Fires continued to rage, and windows burst from their panes without a bomb blast's encouragement. The flames were licking so tempestuously that even the glass needed to dive out of its path.

Curtains, now streaks of flame, danced from open windows, as bricks seemed to glow a deep orange as they stored an incredible amount of heat.

We began to run, as fast as we possibly could, the

sweat dripping off me a result of my efforts, but also down to the awe-inspiring heat that chucked itself from every direction.

"This way!" called Mike, as he tried to guide me through the streets, my hazy vision now blinded by the vibrant colours of a burning town. It was back to the way that I liked it; just Mike and me.

I would have preferred it had it not been the middle of an allied air raid, but there was a security when it was just the two of us, one that had long comforted me.

The comfort seemed to extend to the pain of my injuries; the pounding headache courtesy of Diehl's rifle still present, but not nearly so debilitating. The stars too had begun to fade further, my eyes slowly regaining their focus as if I had been asleep for many days.

My cheek, however, was still pouring blood, the flaps of skin flailing as we pounded through the streets and I could not help but wonder what kind of things Diehl had left in there for me.

At the thought, I wiped at the hole with the back of my sleeve, hoping to get some of the disgusting saliva out of my body. The thought was enough for me to convince myself that I would die, so I quickly filled my mind with anything other than that.

A body suddenly clattered into me, sending me into a pile of bricks that had been hastily swept to one side to keep the road clear. I fell hard, my knee splitting as it crashed into the mountain of pain.

Up ahead, Mike continued to run, his silhouette disappearing into a cloud of dust and smoke.

I looked at the man that had collided into me, who was sobbing over something as he tried to bundle it back into his arms. He had no uniform on, apart from that of a French civilian, and so I felt it my duty to check if he was alright.

"Monsieur," I shouted over the incandescent noise, placing a comforting hand on his shoulder.

He did not register that I was stood with him, instead silently scooping up the object in his arms and turning to run away from all the madness. I felt sorry for him, as I realised what it was, he was so desperate to get away from all of this, but I was certain that his dog had already been killed.

I felt the smoke around me clear as I sucked in huge lungfuls of the stuff, as I charged to catch up with Mike. It threatened to stick in the back of my throat and refused to reinvigorate me, until I was soon choking and spluttering as I ran.

I did not stop though, I could not, and before too long I saw Mike, craning over his shoulder as he sought me out.

"Come on!"

It was only as he shouted that I realised that he had stopped running, and he was waiting for me with a bicycle in hand. He pushed it towards me, and, in unison, we swung our legs over and started to pedal.

We had stashed them behind a large bush that marked the boundary of *Besançon* in the hope that they would help spur us on the final leg of our journey to peace. Jules and Andrew had done the same, on another road, so that the possibility of the bikes being found, or the men for whom they were intended being discovered, was minimised somewhat.

It was a futile attempt at making ourselves feel better, a mild way of suggesting that the Germans were not as clever as we had hoped. But the thought of four bikes hidden in the French countryside, easy to find, but allowing four saboteurs to make haste from the scene of a crime, filled us all with an incredible amount of glee. It was the nearest thing to entertainment that we could get out here.

My knee ached tremendously as my legs bounced up and down, the pedals flying round in circuits until I could keep going no longer. My thighs felt as though acid was burning inside of them and, after a few seconds of rest, I continued on in my fury.

The incline of the road grew slightly, to the point where it would have almost been better if the two of us dismounted and walked up the hill. But it meant that we were nearing our destination, and soon we would be able to stop.

At the thought of making it back to Jules' house, I could not help but want to pedal all the more, as I thought of the small, six-year-old boy who was hopefully in the trench at the bottom of the garden, alongside Christopher.

I wanted so desperately to talk to him, to reassure him that the rest of his war would be different now, that he might possibly be able to go to sleep knowing that this corner of France would no longer be the frontline of a bomber's war.

But most of all I wanted him to know that a repeat of what had happened to him alongside his mother was now all but impossible.

The more that I thought of the young boy's face, the more dread began to creep into my mind. I had seen good fortune and bad in equal measure so far tonight. I only hoped that extended to the bombs that had fallen around Jules' home.

I couldn't bear the thought of seeing Georges' lifeless body, in amongst all the rubble and debris of a wayward bomb that had fallen directly on the house. To cap it all I just knew that Christopher would have somehow survived.

The thought made my legs fly fanatically, overtaking Mike like a horse in the final straight of the Grand National. He called out to me, but there was nothing I could do about it, my mind was totally focused on getting back.

But, within seconds, I realised that the village had been fortunate. No one stirred around here. In fact, not much was stirring anywhere now.

The roar of aircraft engines was now some way off in the distance, as the bombers changed course and took a different path home. The sounds of the roaring flames weren't quite audible, but there was a rumbling undercurrent of continuous noise that told me the inferno was still raging down in *Clerval.*

As I calmed myself down, my legs slowed, as the humanness re-entered them once more. Mike caught up with me.

"What's got into you, old fruit?" he puffed, clapping me on the back.

"I—"

There was a sudden bellow, followed by a beast-like growl and, as I turned around to face the noise, I was filled with wonder and fear in equal measure.

A tall plume of fire and rage erupted over *Sochaux* and illuminated all of its surroundings, as if it was the middle of the day. The light was so bright that I could make out the silhouettes of people, some who had stopped to marvel at what was going on, others far too focused to be distracted.

The orange pillar continued to climb for about two seconds, until it was engulfed by a black cloud that seemed darker than the night air.

Mike began to laugh, a small whoop as he dismounted his bicycle and allowed it to clatter to the ground.

There was a spring in his step and, as much as I hated myself for it, there was one in mine too.

Looking around me, seeing that the place was completely deserted, I too dismounted my bike and joined in with Mike's jubilations. We embraced, slapping one another so hard on the back that I thought the food that I had consumed was about to make a reappearance.

"We did it, old fruit! We've done it!"

I couldn't help but think of Diehl, his remains somewhere in amongst the black cloud that now lingered over the entire town. I almost hated myself for it, but I could not help but feel sorry for him. He wasn't to know that his own greed would be the direct downfall of his death.

If only he hadn't been searching through those pockets.

The emotions that soared through my body were almost as varied as the colours that now permeated the sky; a rich orange of burning flames, a blackness of smoke and dust and a slight hint that the sky would soon be giving way to the morning.

A glimmer of hope.

I couldn't quite believe that we had managed it, with nothing more than a scratch on my cheek as a reminder. Mike too could not comprehend what we had managed to pull off, as he continually told me as he wrapped his arms around me time and time again.

"Come on, let's go," he said eventually, as we took our time in getting back to the house now instead of racing. There was no need for us to. If we were suddenly caught or killed now, we had done what we had come to. We had succeeded.

There was an air of overwhelming triumph as we made it back to the house, Andrew and Jules getting back before us. We shook hands and embraced, even raising a toast to everyone from Cluzet to the King. A party atmosphere was hard to avoid.

"Just one thing," Christopher muttered in the midst of our celebrations, his face stony cold and serious. He lifted his glasses back to his face, his pointed nose sharper than ever before. "Now is the time to be more vigilant than ever. Now is when we simply cannot let our guard down. We have to be more careful than we ever have been before."

There was a moment of contempt for the short, stubby man that had seemed so incompetent. But we all knew that he was right. Sombrely, we took our seats in the chairs dotted around the room and reflected on what we had done.

Yes, we had been successful. But if we could carry on in the fight, then that could be measured as an even bigger triumph. There was no sense in being caught now.

"*Jean,* your face. We should stitch that up." Jules was quick to produce a kit that seemed to have everything in it that he would need, enough to set up his own small hospital. I flinched as he leant in towards me, but not because of the pain.

"In a minute," I muttered leaving the room and using my aching legs once more as I climbed the stairs.

I pushed the door to Georges' room gently, allowing it to softly swing open just enough so that I could poke my head in through it.

I smiled gently as I stared at his face, asleep so soon after the biggest night of his father's life. He was perspiring gently, in only the way that a child can as they engage in a vibrant dream.

His small body was angelic as I stared, and I

couldn't help but allow the tears to fall as I thought about what could have been for my own child.

My heart was full as I watched him, the bedsheets gently rising and falling with his shallow breaths, but at the same time aching. I needed to look away, but I was finding it difficult.

Eventually, after about five minutes of staring, I shut the door, but not before I had whispered one last thing to him, in the hope of it filtering through into his dream.

"You're safe now. Never again."

29

Our plan had been to lie low for as long as possible, until the dust had settled, and the Germans had lost hope in finding the saboteurs. We had made such a mess of one of their most prized occupied possessions, that they were certain to be incandescent that we had managed to get to it.

I had, in the few minutes of sleep that I had managed to steal in amongst all my excitement, dreamt of the rage that the *Führer* himself had flown into at the receipt of such news; glass tumblers and maps thrown into walls and at junior officers who stood nearby.

It was a wonderful dream, made even better by the thought that it was likely to be true.

We had hoped that by keeping our heads down we would evade capture for as long as possible. There had been far too many stories of agents being caught the night after a successful operation, just when the

Germans were at their most vigilant, but also baying for blood.

Staying in Jules' house had allowed us some much-needed rest, and we quickly set to work entertaining ourselves by coming up with new cover stories, and why it was that we were travelling to the places that we were going.

New identities would be conjured up in the coming weeks, as the network of safehouses that we knew existed quickly swallowed us up and protected us until we were completely lost in the thickets of the resistance.

Only then would I be able to relax, and hopefully get more than twenty minutes sleep per night.

As much as coming up with new stories kept us entertained, it was also painfully difficult to sit there as if nothing had happened. It was like being a child on the twenty-sixth of December, Christmas having passed by in a flurry of excitement and happiness. But now, Boxing Day, and nothing stirred, nothing gave off any inkling of the elation that we had recently basked in.

We were all like a coiled spring, a striker ready to slam down on a percussion cap and set off a chain of explosions, and the tension in the house certainly felt like something was brewing.

Nerves were frayed and highly irritable, to the point where areas were reserved for people to withdraw to in the event of an explosion. We could not risk an argument at this stage of the operation. We needed to stay friends for as long as possible.

Jules had been the only one allowed out, on account of the fact that his papers were genuine, and would stand up to the level of scrutiny that the Germans were now no doubt carrying out.

He also had a watertight cover story; his mother lived in *Sochaux*, and he wished to check on her after the previous night's air raid.

But, as he stood before us, he was the object of pure jealousy of all those who sat in his house. He had been able to see all the destruction and confusion that we had caused, but also prod around for any information that might have been of use to us.

The look on his face was ridden with anxiety and paranoia, as the glances over his shoulder, even when stood in his own front room, could testify.

"I have information," he stated as he looked around him.

"Good," I said. "Are you going to tell us?"

He wiped his nose exuberantly with the palm of his hand, almost dislocating it completely in the process. A layer of perspiration had already enveloped over his skin, but his dry, cracked lips spoke of the dehydration that was gripping his body.

"It is from Philippe."

"The police officer?" Mike asked, choking slightly in his desperation to be heard.

"Yes."

"Do you think you can trust him?"

I hadn't been expecting Jules to smile but, when he did, it was as if the apprehension had been blown up with the machines in the factory.

"There are two opposing sides down there in *Clerval* and *Sochaux*. Those who are happy that the factory is gone, and those who are not. Those who are happy have smiles on their faces, a spring in their step. Philippe had perhaps the biggest smile of them all. I am confident which side he is on, my friend."

"Good," Mike said without hesitation. "Then what was his information?"

Jules' face suddenly dropped, the anxiety rising up within him quicker than an express train.

"Down there," he said, motioning to *Sochaux*, "the situation…it is very…volatile. Very dangerous."

"I could have saved you a trip out, Jules. We know it's dangerous. We can feel it from all the way up here."

"Of course," Jules mumbled diligently. He sat down in his chair, his feet rubbing on the floorboards below as if he just had to be moving in some way. Perhaps it made him feel safer.

His hands rubbed one another, massaging the heels of his hands that I could now see were ever so slightly burnt. As I went to ask him how he had incurred such an injury, he began to speak once more, and my desire to hear more from him superseded the want of curing my curiosity.

"The Germans, Philippe supposes *Gestapo*, have already been to see people. They went to Peintre's house first thing this morning. The second that they suspected sabotage. They're trying to do things alone, no assistance from the police, but they could hardly keep something like this under wraps. The entire town is out on the streets in one way or another."

A worried look descended on every face in the room.

"Were you able to get to Peintre?"

"No. Too many soldiers around. Philippe said that he does not think that they would have got anything from him. Not yet, anyway."

"Not yet?" Andrew asked.

"The *Gestapo* took him away this morning. Hasn't been seen since."

There was a silence as we tried not to reminisce of the resistance to interrogation training that we had been put through in Scotland. Peintre wouldn't have stood a chance.

"Then we should suppose that Peintre has already given us up. Worst case scenario and all that."

There was yet another period of reflection as we each wracked our brains, trying to think of anything that had given ourselves away in our limited contact with the factory owner. There was nothing that I could conjure up, but that did not mean that he did not have anything to give to the Germans. He had seen our faces, and, with the right description, our likeness could soon be painted on every street corner in the whole of France.

"Had the Germans been to see anyone else? Any

other suspects?" I asked, trying to keep the fear from fumbling its way into my speech.

Jules had sucked in his lower lip and was biting down on it, hard. It was a bright red colour when it re-emerged. He nodded silently, before taking a few seconds to compose himself. He was doing well, I thought, the way that he was continuing to talk steadily and confidently, despite the fact that what he had gleaned was clearly affecting him tremendously.

"I am worried," he said calmly, but in a matter of fact sense. "For you, you can each disappear. Start new lives and hide. I cannot do that. I have Georges. It will be incredibly difficult for me if they start asking questions."

I had neither the patience nor the desire to see Jules suddenly begin to think of anything other than the matter at hand, even if he was trying to think of what was best for his son.

"Who were the others, Jules? The other suspects. Do you know who they are?"

"A group of workers who did not appear for duty today. They are suspected of the sabotage. There were around thirty of them who did not show today."

"Thirty? Well, I say that number can only be a good thing for us. By the time that they have rounded all them up, I daresay that we will be long gone."

"I wouldn't be so sure," Jules interrupted, clearly put out by Mike's buoyancy in the matter. "Some of that number could possibly have been killed in the raid. The others were probably on orders of Cluzet.

However, I am not sure how long they could hold out."

"Why not?"

"The Germans suppose the workers who committed the sabotage are not in *Sochaux*. So, the authorities cannot get to them quickly. But the people they can get to quickly are still in the town."

"Their families," Christopher muttered, his voice crackled and weak and as if speaking through his nose.

"Exactly. Wives, children, parents, anyone really who might mean anything to them."

Mike muttered something under his breath which wasn't exactly an upbeat endorsement of the Germans' methods.

Christopher began to drum his fingers on the arm of his chair, his breathing laboured and quivering.

"Then we shall have to do something. We simply must. We cannot let these people, these innocent people, suffer while we sit here and watch."

Mike threw a deadly glare his way, "We will sit here, Christopher. And watch if we have to. We are far too valuable to the Germans to compromise our position. If you want to hand yourself over to them, then be my guest. But we're going to be making the best of our situation."

We all wanted to help; it was the natural inhibition of a normal human being to do so. But we each knew that in reality there was no way of doing so. It was going to be awful, but we had to sit tight.

There was nothing else we could do, or so I thought.

"There must be something else that we can do to help them," Christopher urged, the fire in his belly clearly stoked at the prospect of rescuing the defenceless. It was unusual to see him so roused, but his vigour and determination seemed to be nothing more than warm air. A desire to do something, but no idea what.

"What on earth can we possibly do?" I asked, a genuine desire to help the people, but no more of an idea than anyone else on how to go about it. "We simply cannot risk leaving this place. Not now."

"Not now," Christopher repeated, as he coolly rose from his chair, an element of peace washing over him. The clammy skin that had come to characterise his moments of frustration was all but gone, something of a normal pigment returning as the blood began to flow just as much as his ideas did.

He walked around the room, every pair of eyes upon him as his mind whirred. To me, he had always seemed like such a short, stubby little man, with not much of a physical presence that seemed particularly threatening. But, as he strutted about, he seemed to gain at least four inches taller, his chest uncharacteristically puffing out and a confidence that I had not yet seen.

"Not now," he repeated again, wagging his finger. "But at night. We can still move around at night. Am I right in assuming that?"

"To a degree, yes. We will leave this town at night when it comes to it."

"I have an idea. But I am not all that sure how it will work or whether you lot will even agree to it. Would you like to hear it?"

His eyes were ablaze now, his heart almost thumping through the underside of his shirt as he ferociously began to demand our response through a determined glare. This was what this man was good at, finding a solution to a dire situation faced by other people. It was why I was suddenly glad that he was still with us.

"I don't think we have too many other options right now, Christopher. Besides, it's killing us sitting here knowing what's going on."

30

"Blimey," Mike retorted, pleased but equally disgusted. "And I thought you were meant to be a pacifist."

"I still am," Christopher defended, ever so slightly hurt that Mike would call his convictions into question. He looked to me for some kind of support, but I was completely on the same side as Mike. I was quite dumbstruck at the suggestion that had just come out of Christopher's mouth.

What was more, there had been an element of pride to it all, a slight enjoyment over the whole thing, and it was that that was beginning to worry me. Christopher shuffled around on his feet for a moment or two, as we each struggled to come to terms with the change in his character.

He stood impatiently, like a man waiting to hear from a bank manager about his application for a loan. Christopher's was a business proposal like no other.

"When was it, Christopher?" Mike asked, playfully.

"When was what?"

"When was it that you had a brain transplant?"

Mike chuckled heartily, pushing himself back into his chair in disbelief. For some reason, Christopher could not see why we were all so confused at his proposal, not one of us could quite believe it.

We all enjoyed a slight giggle at the remark including, surprisingly, Christopher, who until that very moment had been a man who was content at not taking any entertainment in anything. He had refrained from enjoying the thought of killing the Germans, but he had also abstained from everything else that anyone else could take happiness from; drinking, music, even talking to people at times. He was a complete recluse. But one who had now appeared from his shell, in the most explosive manner possible.

"Frankly, I don't think it matters a jot when I changed and why. The real question that I think we should all try and answer is whether we think we can make it work or not."

The sincerity returned to his face with more gravity to it than ever before, so much so that he looked to me as I expected a judge to look, as he pulled on the black cap of a death sentence. From what I had heard from him so far, it was as if I was looking such a sentence right in the face.

Jules' face was contorted and confused, while Andrew's was being stretched and pulled by his fingers, as he tried to process everything that was going on around him. He looked exhausted, as I was sure all of us did, but his face seemed so full of a puffiness that he almost looked unrecognisable. His eyes, in the brief moment that they appeared from under his hands, were swollen like golf balls, and redder than the side of a London bus. I could do nothing to help him, other than wish with all my heart that his head was still as alert as ever, as we were going to call on every ounce of mental energy that each man had to offer.

There was a prolonged and drawn out silence while we thought our own thoughts for a moment. It was as if we were each going through a period of remembrance, for an object that we each missed terribly and longed to have in our possession once again.

For me, it was peace. That feeling of enjoyment and security that had become so rare. Strangely enough, it wasn't prior to the war that I thought of when thinking of peace. It was that maiden solo flight in the Hurricane that I had long dreamt of; the clouds, the sound of the purring engine and the falling sun that made the sky around me bleed a glorious orange.

"Let me get this straight, I seem to be missing something," Jules announced, interrupting the roaring Merlin and the feeling of total control that only a cockpit of a fighter plane can give you. "Your plan, Christopher, is to leave the safety of this house and go back out. You think there is value in hitting the Germans again, tonight."

"Not just tonight," Christopher interjected. "More than that, we keep going."

"So, we keep going? Keep fighting?" Jules was getting worked up, as he thought about what he had been through already in this war, and what it was that the converted conscientious objector was volunteering him for. His face reddened as he allowed the heat of his own blood begin to get the better of his usual calm and reasonable façade.

"But what is the point in that? Have you not succeeded in what you came here to do? Why would you put yours, and everyone else's lives at risk once again for the sake of riling the Germans up even more? Do you not think about what that might do to them? They are not kind people, if you have not noticed."

"I have noticed," Christopher retorted. "In fact, many of my family members are experiencing first-hand what the Germans are really like. And the fact that a descendent of Jews is taking part in this would rile them even more, I daresay."

Christopher displayed the first signs of what I could only describe as aggression as he paced around the front room, frustrated that he was not met with the grins and enthusiastic welcomes that he had so obviously been expecting.

However, I hated to think it, but Jules had a point.

We were safe where we were. We were useful in our own way by keeping our heads down.

Our long training had, at its core, always been about one thing. Choosing your battles. And we needed to do that more than ever before.

After taking a few seconds to collect his thoughts and allow the boiling blood to return to a gentle simmer, Christopher continued to justify his plan, the one that could easily result in nothing short of a bloodbath.

"Going back out on the attack will keep the Germans on their toes. They'll be expecting us to do exactly what we are doing right now; going to ground and keeping our heads down. If we go back out it'll show that we aren't afraid of them. It'll show them that they have more of a reason to fear us.

"Plus, were we not always told that it is harder to hit a mobile target rather than a stationary one? So why would we sit here and wait for them to come to us?"

His reasoning was sound, rousing almost, and I felt a slight stirring in the pit of my stomach that hinted that I was beginning to come around to his way of thinking. I was starting to allow myself to get fired up again.

"One other thing," Mike suggested, in support of Christopher, "the more attacks that we can scramble together, the more resources the Germans will have to use to protect everything else. That way it means that it is more likely that the families around here will be left alone."

"Yes, for now, anyway," Jules said, adding in his dose of pessimism into the mix. "But then it will not be you who has to deal with the aftermath. It is impossible for dead men to feel remorse for their actions."

There was a period where we all looked at our feet. Jules was right. We were all heading for an early grave, but the people who would be left behind would be forced into an unimaginable turmoil.

"But the people of *Sochaux* are strong. I think they have proved that. If this is what you want to do, then do not let me stand in the way. I would suppose that you would have a very large number of supporters around here that will have more smiles on their faces when they see more attacks."

Christopher smiled slightly, nodding gently and bringing a palm to rest on Jules' back.

"Thank you, Jules. We will need more than just those that are in this room," Christopher said. "Do you think there is a possibility you will be able to raise more men to assist us?"

"Not just men, my friend. Women too, some children would almost certainly help if given the opportunity."

"Good. That's that sorted then. We just need some additional targets. From what I have seen and heard some rascals took out the factory. So, I doubt that would be a legitimate target."

"The telephone exchanges. There's one to the east of the town, another just on the outskirts to the south. Both of them would do as targets."

Mike rose from his chair, pulling the map of the surrounding area from behind a row of books on the top shelf of a bookcase in the corner. Laying it out triumphantly across the table, he pointed at two marks, as we all gathered around it excitedly.

"The railway yard here too. We've hit it before, but they would have restocked," I muttered, my warm breath disgusting those around me as they backed away from the map.

We spent the next fifteen minutes coming up with even more targets, places that weren't exactly vital to the German war effort, but valuable to them, nonetheless. The bonus of picking these non-vital targets was that they were not as well defended, essentially easy targets for us.

"Gather your men together then, Jules. And we'll come up with a more solid plan. We'll go again tonight."

We were all even more exhausted now that the last ounce of brain power had been sapped by the excitement. But each man had a fire behind his eyes, one so well-fuelled that they would burn for at least another twenty-four hours. I was just hoping that they would be able to plod along again for another few hours after that.

~

"THAT IS OUR PLAN. What we need from you is a commitment," a few heads nodded prematurely before I had even finished my statement. "We need a commitment from you that you will keep on going, keep on finding and attacking targets until you get to the very last of your supplies. I want you to build a campfire beneath a motorcycle if that is what it takes. Just keep on going."

There were more than just a few excited eyes now looking at me. Some of them had been waiting since the first day of occupation to get back at the Germans, and now here was a British agent suddenly giving them the go-ahead to do so.

From what I could see, there was a dedicated band of courageous souls in front of me, some of the bravest that I had ever had the pleasure to have known. I took a dredge of their confidence from them, but also a scepticism that any of this would work. The pessimism was fuelled by the thought that each man who had volunteered for such a job must also have been just as stupid as they were brave.

"Once you have completely exhausted your supplies, you must disperse. Two or three men should be a maximum. The smaller the group, the better your chances of getting away."

Each one of them looked back at Mike with a waxy, blank expression etched into their faces. Not one of them was genuinely preparing to make it back alive. All those who had wished to do so had shrunk back into the shadows when approached by Jules. I didn't blame any of them.

The rest of the evening passed by in silence, a few men sharing cigarettes but not much else. I felt a pain in my heart as Jules reappeared from putting Georges to bed. There was not much of a plan in place for what would happen if he was killed, but Georges had enough common sense about him to go about searching for a new adoptive parent.

The sun seemed to take an age to set, the sky even longer to surrender the final few rays of light, but eventually the hour appeared, but no one seemed keen to admit it.

"That's time then gents," Mike eventually muttered, rising to his feet. "Group one, prepare to leave."

Five men bundled their belongings and weapons together and made for the door.

Three more groups until I was due out.

The minutes ticked by.

31

The telephone exchange that sat a few miles west of *Besançon* was not all that impressive. In fact, had there not been pristine glass and the occasional movement inside, one could have mistaken it for a dilapidated old hut in the middle of an unknown forest.

But, to us, as we lay in amongst the long, overgrown brambles and weeds of the forest floor, it presented our next target.

The hut itself was in a curious place, a road running from north to south connecting the exchange to two more villages, the east side overlooking a large valley and the west, where Mike and I were perched, loomed large over the top. The bank that sloped steeply towards the shed took a fantastic amount of sunlight, the grass around us so green and luscious that it looked almost envious of the rest of the forest.

Laying on my back on the slope, my feet towards the building, I felt quite content, allowing myself to become immersed in the slight movements of the trees and the glimmering stars, as they played a game of hide and seek in amongst the leafy canopy.

There was a faint, musky light coming from inside the hut, from what I presumed was a small electric lamp hanging somewhere on the ceiling. It was cold where I was, but I knew that I would soon be moving, but the poor souls inside were expected to sit where they were for hours on end. I hoped that it would all play to our advantage when the time was right.

There was a mutual silence between Mike and me, but I was glad for it. I was glad also that once again things were just down to us, as I knew that I could depend on him to do the right thing when the starting pistol sounded.

From what we had observed in the hour or so since we had been concealed in the undergrowth, there would be at least two people in the building. There was an element of guesswork to be made but, we had seen one man lighting a cigarette as he took in the evening air, calling back to another somewhere in the shed. One man talking to another made two, unless he was some kind of psychopath.

I felt anxious, my heart fluttering impatiently and my mouth suddenly drying up of any liquid that I had. I was gagging for a drink, so much so that it became all I could think about, even when the silence of the swaying branches was interrupted by some laughter.

It was a deep, throaty laugh, how I imagined a

lion to laugh if they could have done such a thing. The laugh was fused with the sound of a latch clicking shut, the door closing behind the man as he stepped out onto the small veranda at the front of the hut.

We both watched silently, as the man's face was illuminated by a striking match, his collar patch briefly lit up to reveal two grey bars that flickered gently in the light. The match went out, but the tip of the cigarette continued to burn fiercely, a glowing orange that matched the intake of breath of the soldier.

Mike nudged me inadvertently as he drew out his pistol from one pocket, and a magazine from the other. Like an eager younger brother, I began to do the same.

I was careful to slide the magazine into the well first time, so that I did not accidentally clink on the side of the grip, or scrape clumsily into place. It slipped in without protest and I made sure to give it a gentle tap from the bottom to make sure that it was in place. The last thing that I wanted was to pull the trigger only to watch the magazine drop from under my grip.

I felt Mike do the same as me, as we both pinched firmly at the top of our weapons and dragged the top slides back until there was a soft, but easily audible click, akin to when a dry twig snaps under the weight of an advancing man.

Together the three of us, Mike, me and the

soldier, all stopped. The cigarette hovered in the air for a moment, a dull glow just about visible, while the two of us gently eased the top slides back into place.

We listened for a few moments more, wondering if it was our weapons that had made the noise or whether we had an unwanted visitor sneaking up behind us. Normally, if we had been able to set up an observation post, we would have taken the time to rig up some kind of early warning system, a bunch of leaves or two tin cans rigged up to a piece of string. But there had been no time for that tonight. We were going in as primitive as possible.

As I eased back the top slide once more, confident that the burning cigarette was back up at the man's lips, I could not help but wonder how many more times I would have to do this. I had inspected hundreds of weapons now, preparing to engage in combat with the persistent thought that each step could well be my last.

It took its toll on a man, to such an extent that nothing short of a complete cessation of hostilities would be able to reinvigorate the mind. It felt as though my body had not slept properly for months, which was probably down in no small part to the fact that I hadn't. I longed for a proper rest, one where I could completely close my eyes without having to think where the nearest weapon was or the closest escape route.

But the longer I stayed out there, lying down in forests and sneaking around factories, the closer I came to achieving a complete rest, one that I knew I would never wake from. As we prepared to slip down the bank, it was a prospect that wasn't completely disregarded anymore. It was a thought that I had often welcomed.

Slowly, we moved down the bank, all kinds of prickles and thistles embedding themselves in my buttocks as we slipped our way towards the shed. My trousers began to flap around as I realised that I had torn the fabric, and that a stream of cool air was circulating around my limbs that wasn't as unwelcome as I had first thought.

We were going to have to get a move on, if we wanted to stand a chance of taking out the first soldier before he returned back inside. He had already turned his back on us to look down at the valley below, which was completely motionless and full of an inky blackness like that of an inkwell. I could not imagine what it was that he was looking at, but he had already ceased to lift the orange tip to his mouth, instead flicking it somewhere around his feet for his boot to finish off.

I pulled my knife from the small sheath that I had strapped to the inside of my jacket, its well-polished and recently sharpened surface just glinting in the moonlight momentarily. Quickly, I hid from any source of light, instead keeping it close to my chest as I pulled myself down by the heels of my shoes.

Hitting the ditch at the bottom of the bank, Mike was quickly on his feet and gliding towards the hut, his feet dancing around the gravel and somehow avoiding making too much noise. I followed, slower than he but just as quietly, as we fixed our eyes on the man that was now leaning over the bannister on the other side of the veranda.

It was going to need to be quick and ruthless, as we were going to be immediately disadvantaged the second we made any noise over that of a normal woodland mouse. Pressing my body into the veranda, I laced my fingers together to make a stirrup for Mike to step into. As if he was simply mounting a horse, he stepped in, swung his leg over the bannister and thumped down onto the other side.

There were two loud, heavy footsteps that thumped over the wood as he lunged towards the soldier, while I ran around to the far side to make use of the stairs.

By the time I reached the top of the four or so stairs, Mike was already embroiled in a rather fierce fist fight with the man, as he struggled to embed his knife into the fellow as he had planned.

Instead, they fell to the floor tussling and turning as each one tried to gain the upper hand. Mike was refusing to use his pistol, for now, instead preferring the softer approach of a knife, while the German was struggling with the catch on his leather holster down by his hip. If he got that pistol out, then it was game over for Mike.

There was a sudden grunt, as the German managed to land a nice square fist on Mike's jaw somewhere, which was followed by a furious roar, similar to the laugh, but the tone far more murderous in its intent.

"*Hilfe!*" he screamed, half a second before an ear-splitting bang, and the sound of light matter slowly sticking to the ground around us. The screaming figure fell to one side, and I could just about make out the heaving chest of Mike, as his pistol was still levelled at where the German's chest had been seconds before.

Not waiting for gravity to do its work, Mike heaved the body to one side, thumping so loudly on the wooden veranda that I thought it might fall through.

Instead, the body remained motionless, as the two of us set to work quickly, and as loudly as we now liked.

I took the lead, using my shoulder to smash into the door, the latch spinning off its mountings and falling to the ground.

Inside was nothing too spectacular, just one large room with a few amenities to make the night pass a little quicker for the poor souls posted out there.

A single lightbulb was the only source of light, hanging precariously from the ceiling in the middle, swaying gently as it sensed the urgency and excitement that was in the air.

A figure was already up from his chair, trying desperately to retrieve his pistol from the leather belt that he had removed, and rested atop one of the tables.

He pulled it out just in time but was unable to raise it quick enough for me.

"*Nein!*" I screamed, surprised at the maliciousness in my throat. "*Hände! Hände!*" I bellowed at the top of my lungs several times over, praying desperately that he would do as I said and simply show me his hands. But I wasn't holding out much hope.

I caught sight of the single stripe on the German's sleeve denoting that he was a lance corporal, and probably in charge of the whole operation here this evening. It wasn't going all that well for him, and he knew that if he was to simply let us have our way, his life would not be worth living once his superiors found out.

So, he did what any decent soldier would have done. He quickly raised his arm, bringing the pistol up towards my eyes and I could tell that he had already taken up first pressure on the trigger. One gentle squeeze would now be all that it took to have my life snatched away from me.

But he was marginally too slow. I squeezed harder and faster than he was able to, my pistol already well-aimed and ready.

The back of his head exploded, as the round entered just above his eye and took bits of skull and eye socket with it as it travelled through. There was a short silence, followed by a slow trickling of what sounded like water as his body slumped to the ground.

There was a precious, harmonious silence for what felt like a minute or two, which was glorious as I basked in it. But then, my body was shocked into action once again, when an incredible scream threatened to sound louder than any of the gunshots had done.

32

Until that moment in time, I had not noticed the young girl who was in the room, perhaps only nineteen or twenty years of age. She sat in an uncomfortable-looking wooden chair, in front of a series of switches and plugs, with wires poking out of everywhere that I could see. It was a wonder that she had even known what had gone on around her as she would have had to concentrate so hard on what she was doing.

The headset that was wrapped around her ears, a microphone bending round in front of her mouth, had become skewed by her brash movements.

She continued to scream, a heart-wrenching, pained cry, my ears starting to ring under the strain of it all. Mike instantly went to comfort her, his arms wrapped around her face, bloodied by the spraying shrapnel of the dead soldier.

Her cries turned to sobs but were drowned out as

she wept into the crook of Mike's arm, the blood running from her face and into the fibres of Mike's clothes. Her body shook violently, as if she was possessed, as Mike made uncharacteristic soothing noises to try and comfort her as best as he could.

I noticed by her clothes that she was nothing more than an ordinary civilian, perhaps one just as fed up with all the death she had seen in her own hometown. With two German soldiers to protect her, she probably would have assumed that she would have been relatively safe out here in the forest.

As her head rocked back from Mike's arms, her weeping still continuing but somewhat under control, I could not help but look at her bloodied and gory face and freeze. It was a face that I had seen before, one that I had taken time to admire and appreciate.

It was Suzanne.

But I knew that it couldn't be. The face was too young, the girl too innocent and weepy to have been the woman that had been alongside me fighting the Germans. I tried to cut away but found it increasingly difficult to do so.

"Jean! The charges. Now! Come on, quickly!"

Even after Mike's screams I was finding it difficult to move naturally, the sudden leap of my heart still taking its time to return to its normal pattern. But slowly I was able to make my body move, as I swung my back round and caught the satchel as it slid around my waist.

Opening the flap, I revealed all the goodies and treats that I had for Mike, like Father Christmas.

Mike dove in, with so much enthusiasm and vigour that I thought he was about to jump headfirst into the bag and disappear. He began pulling out the charges that I had become so used to seeing, with additional 808 that he intended to put in every little crevice that he could. We wanted a big bang, but not only that, we wanted to ensure that we completely destroyed the switchboard.

No phone calls in or out of *Besançon* for the foreseeable future was one that filled me with a tremendous excitement.

As Mike continued with the explosives, I began rummaging around the few tables that were there, discarding newspapers and playing cards in search of something far more rewarding. I found a notebook with various dates and numbers on that I could not quite translate quick enough, so instead bundled it into my satchel in preparation for the return journey.

Finding nothing of any real significance, I staggered outside, hurriedly pulling the body of the soldier into the hut from outside and propping him next to his comrade.

"Ready. Delays are set. Time to go!"

"What about her?" I asked, nodding towards the still distraught young girl.

"What about her?" Mike replied, shrugging. "Leave her be. She'll work out soon enough that the best place to be is as far away from here as possible."

"We can't just leave her here though."

"Why not? She's not our problem, Jean. Come on, let's go."

She had bundled herself into a ball, gripping tightly to her knees and allowing bloody tears to roll down her cheeks. Staring into her pretty, but forlorn eyes, I spoke as slowly and as clearly as I possibly could.

"You need to get out of here. Go home. Quickly. Get away from here. Do you understand?"

She stared back at me, listening but not registering.

"It's no use, Johnny. Come on, let's get gone."

He practically pulled me out of the door and down the steps, my feet slipping in the pool of blood that had been left by the first soldier.

By the time I had reached the bottom of the stairs, I was resigned to the fact that the girl was the master of her own fate. She knew what she had to do to survive, it was down to her if she was going to act on it.

I turned and started to run back the way that we had come earlier on, with far less finesse and elegance as before.

I had just made it to the other side of the track when I heard a frantic and impassioned cry from the hut.

"*Hey! Hey, attendez!*" the girl started screaming, her face dripping with just as much blood as it did sweat.

"Give me strength!" Mike bellowed as I stood up

from the ditch and waved her over. "Can't she make up her mind?!"

Mike's last few words were swallowed up by the first few rapports of gunfire, as they began to zip down the road and kick up the bits of gravel and dust that hissed and whined as they were disturbed.

"Argh!" he screamed, as he slid his body down into the bottom of the ditch, just out of sight of the automatic gunfire that had suddenly ripped through the night. It was a safe bet, in the dark, but not one that would have covered us with much glory.

Rifles and submachine guns started kicking off from every available space up ahead of us, some of the rounds flying dangerously close to my head and making an awful noise as they did so.

The weapons started discharging a lot closer than they had done before and, as I peeked my head up out of the ditch, all I could see were twinkling flashes as they slowly advanced on our position.

I could not see the girl, I could not even see the shed, but I could hear the rounds striking the side and wondered whether they even knew what it was they were aiming at. Hundreds, if not thousands of rounds had already been wasted, and I took quite a confidence in the fact that neither of their two targets had yet been hit. But I worried about one or two lucky rounds that somehow penetrated the thin wood of the shed, prematurely detonating the charges and showering us all in a deadly bomb of glass and shrapnel.

It wouldn't be such a bad way to go though.

I found myself glaring at a petrified pair of white eyes, as they switched on and off as they blinked. Mike was fearful, of that much I was sure, but it was only as I looked at him that I was overcome by a curious sense of the same feeling.

It wasn't a fear that I had experienced before, but more one of resignation that now was my time to go. It was different to how I had imagined it; I had often thought of it as a paralysing and limiting fear, but this one was filling me with a determination to continue to the bitter end. I wanted as many of these Germans to be glaring glassy-eyed to the heavens as I possibly could, before I ended up doing the exact same.

My means were limited, but determination was boundless.

The anguished cry began to register in my head above the din of incoming rounds, which Mike was now beginning to reply to. For a moment or two, the attention was diverted away from the hut and towards the one fool who was trying to take on an entire platoon with one measly pistol.

It just so happened that that fool was lying next to me, a grin now on his face as he relished in the chance to go down fighting. This was what all the comics were full of back at home. Now he was living it.

The screams of the young girl were beginning to become too much for my heart to bear. All I could think of was how helpless Suzanne had been that first time when she had been blown up. Without Mike or me, she would have been dead. That girl was in exactly the same position. I knew that I had to help her.

"Mike! I need to get to her. Can you keep firing while I get her across?"

"Then what?"

"We'll get back up the bank as best we can. Make for the high ground and hope for the best!"

He looked at me sternly, as his body jolted in response to the impacts in the bank just above our ditch.

"If hope is all we've got left, old fruit, then I'd say we're done for this time!"

"Me too. But let's go down fighting, shall we?"

"Absolutely."

I exhaled.

"Right then, after three. One, two—"

But before I could get to the end of my countdown, the girl screamed, louder than before, tearing at all the chords in her throat and bursting a blood vessel or two in her head. She took a few paces backwards, before charging towards us, her eyes fixed on mine as she gathered pace.

I glared dumbfounded as she got closer but, just as her body emerged from the cover of the hut, her right shoulder was ripped backwards, as if an invisible hand had gripped her from behind.

She then spun to the ground where another lucky round ripped into her knee, the sound of her kneecap shattering, clear above all the noise and confusion, making me wince awfully.

"No!" I screamed, repeated by Mike as he hollered at me to leave her.

I scrambled from the ditch, the ground a hotbed of activity and noise, my clothes ripping along with my skin as I skidded down by her side. She was alive, just about and, as she was still close to the shed, I gripped her by her wrists and pulled with all my might.

Rounds began to increase in their density, and I could make out the distinctive noise of them burying themselves inside the dry and arid ground.

The girl's screams had ceased.

I pulled her upright and propped her up against the shed, but there was nothing left in her eyes. They were already glazed and sad, the warm blood oozing out of her chest and leg complemented by the holes that had been ripped open in her arms, stomach and ankle.

She was gone.

I hadn't been able to save her. And there was a decreasing chance that I would be able to save myself.

The road ahead of me was now spitting so furiously that it looked like a pan of water that had been left far too long to boil. There had been little chance of me making it across there unscathed before, but now it was all but impossible.

I made eye contact with Mike as I finished emptying my magazine towards the advancing winks of light.

There was no heartfelt plea to try and get across,

no agonised goodbye as we resigned ourselves to death. Just a slight nod, accompanied by the very daintiest of smiles.

"Good luck, Johnny!" came the call, as he used up the final few rounds in his possession.

"See you back in London!" I called back towards him. "Good luck," I screamed. "…Old fruit," I shouted with both a hint of sadness and amusement.

I had hated being called it but shouting it towards him made me feel ten times better, as I watched his beaming smile disappear as he began to scrabble up the bank.

Now, I was on my own.

33

The gunfire grew to the point where I thought my head would no longer be able to cope, the pressure building inside so great that my skull simply wanted to explode. Part of me wanted to let it.

But I knew that I had to keep going, particularly as I was now all alone in the world, with no one to tell me to pick my feet up and carry on. I would have to simply motivate myself.

Having watched Mike's back dance up the bank as he scurried away in search of freedom, I turned my back to him and charged towards the valley on the far side of the hut. I had totally run out of all options.

There was no chance of charging down the road away from the Germans, as there would surely be reinforcements moving towards me in the next few seconds. My route across the track back towards Mike was blocked by a wall of ammunition, and there was certainly no way that I was about to walk towards my attackers with my white pants on a stick, in submission to the evil occupiers that I had spent so long trying to avoid.

My only hope was the valley, the inkwell of darkness, with a wish that I would simply be swallowed up in the blackness, to at least buy myself some time from my pursuers. But I had put my chances of surviving the drop at less than fifty percent, and even then, I was being generous to myself.

I leapt over the edge, my feet out in front of me and the underside of my body tensed and ready for the impact. But, even still, the force was so great that I felt as though great chunks had been taken from my legs and, as I started to slide my way down into the valley, I could already feel the blood being left in a long trail behind me.

I hit every single groove and bump on the way down, and I felt a certain snap as my foot snagged in a rabbit warren, the momentum behind me cracking my shin in two as I continued to fall to the bottom.

No noise came from my mouth, the initial landing enough to knock the wind from my lungs and prevent me from screaming or grunting any further. The only noise that I could hear was the incredible rush of wind, like I was about to take off, and the sounds of my body impacting everything that got in its way.

In the darkness, it was difficult to make anything out until it was too late, and it was especially so with the tree, its vague outline slowly being filled in as I hurtled towards it. I tried to wriggle and roll to one side, but it was advancing too quickly, and I immediately knew that I had made it so much worse for myself.

By trying to wriggle from its path, I had lined up the base of the trunk perfectly with the bridge of my nose.

I felt the impact, but not much else after that.

IT WAS ONLY as the rain slowly began to smack me on the cheek, like a rude awakening from my mother, that I realised that I was still alive. My nose, crumpled and tender, was surrounded by brown, flaking blood, that fell off in large chunks as I gently brushed all around it. Surprisingly though, there was very little blood to tell of my ordeal.

My head, on the other hand, pounded as if to make up for the lack of visible distress, a headache like no other that blinded me as much as it did incapacitate. I ran my hands around my skull, checking for any obvious signs of fracture or dislocation, but I could feel nothing.

I would get over it all, I would just have to soldier on for now. I couldn't lie in the bush forever.

As the rain grew in intensity, I lifted my face to the heavens, allowing the great beads of water to pass over my face, and gently cleanse me.

Thankfully, I had studied maps of the area which the telephone exchange had been in, and so I knew exactly where the bed of the valley would take me.

I started to trudge towards a row of huts I could see some three hundred yards away, covered in a mist on account of the rain, and knew that the sheep would not mind me sheltering in there for an hour or two.

The sky was dark, but a slightly paling of the sky had started and, as I looked at my watch, completely smashed and destroyed, I reasoned that the charges should have gone off some time ago.

But there was no hope of going to check. I possessed neither the courage, nor the energy to ascend the valley drop once again to make sure. Either way, we had inconvenienced the Germans, and that was enough for me.

But I could not help but wonder how the others had fared. We had certainly had a rough night, but we had known that it wouldn't have been easy. I prayed briefly that they had got on alright, and that my head would soon stop pounding as aggressively as it was.

I rested as best as I could in the disused sheep shed, not sleeping exactly, but just allowing my eyes to take it in turns to close momentarily.

I washed in a bucket of rancid water that must have been stagnant for at least a decade, but helped my appearance tremendously by ridding myself of the remainder of the dried blood, the muck and dirt that had stuck to me during my tumble.

Shortly after I began to make my way back to the village, specifically back to Jules' house. It was there that I hoped to find my respite, hoping that Mike had made it back before me along with all the other happy faces.

It did not take me long to find my bearings and, despite the deep bruises that I could feel pressuring my limbs at every pace, I made good time.

I checked my useless watch once more as I set eyes on Jules' home for what felt like the first time in forever.

I was filled with a contentment that I never thought possible. For some reason the fear, the pain that I had gone through, was what I had come to enjoy. It was in these moments, in the immediate aftermath that I took most of my gratification. I felt more alive than ever before.

I relaxed significantly when I saw the front door of Jules' house, even more so when I saw that there was a light on in the front room. I resisted the urge to put my head in my hands there and then and to break down into tears.

I knew in that moment that I needed to stop, at least for a little while, and that vague light that was on somewhere in the house was the only sign that I needed to confirm that I was going to get that.

Ecstasy began to surge through my muscles as I leapt towards the door, a beaming smile hard to conceal.

As normal, I went to push the door open, expecting it to be unlocked as it had been hundreds of time before. But instead, I was met with resistance. The door was still locked.

I presumed that Jules and the others were merely being extra vigilant and, as I wearily flung the door knocker about two or three times, I felt as though I would be crawling through the door on my hands and knees. I withstood the temptation, and instead stood up tall and proud, to make sure that no one could perceive me as weak when they answered the door.

I heard the locks behind the door slide and clunk into place, before it was slowly opened with nothing more than a soft squeak.

But the face that answered the door was not Jules', nor was it Mikes'. At first, I thought that I did not recognise it at all, but after a second or two, I realised who it was. The initial thought that went through my mind was one of hopefulness; I hoped that he hadn't noticed the moment that I had recalled his face.

It was pointed, vermin-like and the chin was all but non-existent. His mouth was small and looked as though he wouldn't have even been able to get a pea into it without being inconvenienced. His eyes were dark and soulless, and the moles that ran down one side of his face were curiously in line with his brows, his nostrils and his lips.

It was a face that I had seen before, and one that I had repulsed the first time around.

It was Murky. SS *Obersturmbannführer* Franz Mökhen.

He looked odd dressed in his civvies, quite as if he had been a man that had spent so many years in uniform that he had forgotten how to hold himself the second that he stepped back out into the normal man's world. His lips curled and unfurled at the rate of four times a minute.

There was a moment shared between us of perhaps ten to fifteen seconds as we both quietly hid our looks of surprise. The German officer was shorter than me, quite considerably, to the point where his pistol, raised at his own midriff height, had a better chance of hitting me in the crown jewels than anywhere else.

"Monsieur Hameur?"

"*Non*," I answered truthfully. "Pelletier."

"Inside please, Monsieur…Pelletier," he growled, a hint of uncertainty in his voice.

I knew that the game that I had played so well for so long was almost up. I had little choice but to do as he had said.

As I stepped inside, the pistol following my every move, I gave myself an internal dressing down at having been such an incompetent fool. The locked door should have served as every indicator that I had needed to have run as far away from Jules' home as I dared, but I had been too exhausted, too arrogant to have done so. I wondered how many others had made it to the door, only for them to turn around and walk away.

"Would you mind," I asked politely and submissively, "putting that thing away? It's terribly dangerous to wave those things about, you know."

I tried to play the obliging and innocent civilian, one who had merely popped round to see his friend and instead was being held at gunpoint.

He glared at me, his eyes widening as he produced a card, which I duly took.

"Ah, I do apologise, *Obersturmbannführer.* What can I do for you?"

I already knew that I was faced with an SS officer but seeing his identity card seemed to make my stomach sink further than it already had been. Nevertheless, I tried to buoy myself with the knowledge that he could have already buried a load of rounds through my heart.

While I was still breathing, I should remain upbeat.

"Monsieur Hameur was arrested last night. He was caught just outside the town with weapons on his possession. Would you happen to know anything about that?"

"No, not at all, I am afraid. I was just passing and thought I would see my old friend. I had heard his wife had died and—"

"Alright. Alright," Murky said, waving his arms around and lowering the pistol, motioning me to enter the living room.

I did so, with a cursory glance up the staircase, half expecting to see the petrified little eyes of Georges looking down towards me. I hoped to the heavens that the little boy had more sense than me and had managed to escape this house with his freedom intact.

I could hear no noise from upstairs. I had to take it as a good sign.

Murky continued to talk to me, as if he had been quite taken in by the story that I was just a passing friend. He asked me questions about how long I had known Jules, how we had met and all the other kind of questions an investigating officer would ask, if someone had just turned up on the doorstep of a criminal.

I passed all the tests and, in a moment of silence where he was thinking of his next question, I decided to take a little more of a handle on the situation and grip it tighter.

I got up from my chair, pointing towards the glasses and bottles that ran along the top shelf of Jules' cabinet.

"Mind if I have a drink? I'm parched."

"No. Go ahead."

"Would you like one? It is not every day that someone like me gets to share a drink with an SS officer," I projected with a playful chuckle.

"No. Not for me thank you. I hope you understand but owing to the situation, and the timings, I would like for you to accompany me back to my headquarters for an…interview."

"Of course."

I felt his eyes shuffle around hastily as I got to the shelf behind him, his body swivelling just to make sure that I wasn't about to make a run for it. His finger twitched towards his pistol once again.

I made a variety of noises, picking up a glass and pretending to peruse the selection of wines that Jules had stored in the cabinet.

I stared myself in the eyes as they came to rest on one bottle in particular. My eyes were heavy and, even in the darkness of the bottle, I could tell how bloodshot they were.

This is your last chance. One final throw of the dice.

Anything you do would be better than being taken in for interrogation.

I thought I made out the swish of fabric as he turned back to face his front, as the scratching nib of his pencil on paper continued to waggle away as he made more notes.

Now was my chance.

I spun, as hard as my aching legs would allow, the bruises threatening to burst and spray blood all over the floor.

I gripped the neck of the bottle so hard that I thought it would smash, as I pulled it high above my head, allowing the fury and rage to course through my veins.

The bottle connected with the back of the German's head spectacularly, the bottle shattering, its red liquid disseminating wonderfully all over the place.

Murky tumbled forward, falling from his chair and onto his knees, stunned at what had happened. But I had messed up.

The force with which I had brought the bottle down on his head was not enough to kill him, it was not even enough to knock the fellow out.

Within moments, he was already scrabbling to his feet and pointing his pistol towards me.

I lunged at him, the jagged neck of the bottle still in my grip and the only thing that I had that resembled any sort of a threat to the German. I watched as his pistol erupted and kicked back six, maybe seven times as I threw myself over the chair towards him.

The gunshots shocked my body, causing me to lose grip on the bottle neck, and I could have almost given up as I heard it tinker to the ground and roll under a chair.

I wondered for a fleeting moment who had taught him to shoot, as every single round missed me by a mile, despite the fact that it would have been harder than to hit me. The sound of glass shattering as more wine bottles were pierced and hunks of plaster were ripped from the walls began to shout all around me, until Murky's weapon jammed, just at the right moment.

He looked down at his weapon, before looking back up to me. That brief glance was all I needed, flying at him shoulder first and bundling him to the ground.

He began to strike me over and over again with the grip of his pistol, as if the headache that I was already battling was not bad enough. But the pain was secondary, the only thing that I could focus on was getting out of the clutches of the German.

He rolled on top of me, striking me so fiercely that I felt my jaw crack and a few teeth become dislodged. I spat them back at him into his face, the blood-infused spittle clinging to his face as he started growling at me.

Suddenly, his weight lifted, as he pulled me up by my neck, the back of my head burying into his snarling mouth as he forcefully applied the pressure.

I lost all control of my body as I fought for breath, my natural reaction of pulling his forearm away from my throat doing nothing to help me to survive. My legs bucked and kicked, but not in the way that I had told them to, as the stars began to burst in my eyes and the room suddenly darkened terrifically.

He knew he was winning, and he began to laugh a manic howl as he smelt the stench of urine as I completely lost control of my bowels. It wasn't fear that had made me do it, just a complete focus on doing one thing to the neglect of everything else; breathing.

The more that Murky began to laugh, the more I could feel the sun setting on my life. I knew that I had one last chance to make it out of this situation alive.

Thankfully, my mind still functioned as it always had done, and I could think back to Arisaig. I was able to think back to my training.

I closed my eyes, saving the one final sense that seemed to be working and reinvesting my energy elsewhere. Instead of the natural urge to get the pressure off my throat, I allowed him to continue, keeping my head as still as possible to let him think that he was winning.

I stretched my arms out below my waist, flattening my palm to make the antithesis of a fist and tensing every bone in my hand ready for impact.

Without giving it much more thought, more because I was running critically low on time than any other factor, I began to work through the one thing that I had learned that I wished I would never have to implement.

I lurched to one side, without much effect other than a tightening around my neck, but it didn't matter all that much now anyway. I was dead regardless, and a tighter grip meant that I could expect death quicker.

But my movement had displaced the German and had opened up his stomach just an inch or two, and that was all that I now needed.

Spinning with all my might, I thrust the heel of my hand into his stomach hard, just under where I imagined his ribs to be, and pushed upwards, as hard as I possibly could. The aim was to apply such a force to his internal organs that he would be in such an excruciating pain that he would simply have to release his grip.

It was dirty fighting, but the Germans had become the masters of it.

There was a satisfying sucking noise as the German tried desperately to provide his battered organs with as much oxygen as possible to make sure that he stayed alive. Unfortunately, he was able to maintain his consciousness.

However, he staggered backwards, clattering into the cabinet and knocking a host of glasses and plates all over the floor with a great noise.

His eyes had rolled into the back of his head and he clutched earnestly at his stomach, clearly in a great pain. He was completely bewildered.

I thought for a moment about finishing him off there and then, but realised that his weapon was jammed, and I could spend longer looking for a weapon of my own than I could really care for.

I was in a bad way too and needed to get out of the situation as soon as possible.

We both gasped for the shared oxygen around us, both bodies demanding for it in order to stay alive.

"Sortez. Sortez…" he gasped hopelessly, as he caught sight of me staggering around and wondering what to do with him.

I decided that I did not need to be prompted again. I stumbled to the back door, my feet crunching on broken glass and china, Jules' living room a complete state, but I doubted that he would be spending too much time in there in the coming days.

I made it to the back door where, by leaping over a fence in the garden, I could traverse across the fields and find the river that would lead me to the next village.

Coughing and spluttering, I staggered across the field, ever conscious that a certain German may have suddenly been able to clear his pistol.

34

The mud had been churned to a sticky mess by the deluge that had started to pour down upon me, making it near enough impossible for my tired and weary legs to lift the extra foot or so to get proper clearance as I staggered.

My squelching footsteps were unprogressively slow and on more than one occasion I nearly sacrificed my boots to the sucking mud that seemed intent on slowing me down even further. Every ounce of energy that I possessed went into making sure that I continued to move, but I knew that if anyone had been able to give chase, it would take them a matter of seconds until they were drawing up close to me.

It was hard work, but something inside was driving me on.

I wasn't entirely sure what it was, but I kept my head up as much as I could and, before too long and through the slight haze that the pouring rain was creating, I could just about make out the ripples landing spectacularly on the otherwise slow-moving river. Just beyond that, on the other side of the bank, would be the vague outlines of buildings.

I knew that if I was able to get there, a feat in itself, then someone would be able to take me in, hide me and take care of me until I could muster up the energy to move on elsewhere.

My confidence, however, was sapped, as well as my energy, and the thought of simply giving up was one that I was constantly battling against.

I had no idea how any of the others had fared, or where they even were. If I was to make it to the next village, there was no guarantee that my contact would be able to help me to the extent that I needed. We had no wireless set, no way of communicating with London to let them know that I was alive, and one of the most senior SS officers in the area had been able to get a good long look at my face.

My prospects of a safe return home after the war had dwindled drastically.

I focused my attention on simply making sure that one foot plunged into the sopping mud after the other, which somehow had the effect of keeping my mind somewhat buoyant considering my situation. It was when I tried to think ahead, to guess at what might come next, that the clouds above me seemed to darken and poured even more rainwater on the excruciating pain inside my head.

Despite the prospect of clean clothes and a nice

warm bed, I was aware that my pace was slowing, to the point where even a snail would more than likely beat me to the river. I grunted and grimaced as the aches and pains of my muscles really began to get the better of me, and I slowly realised that exhaustion could be the end of me.

I tried to shout, in the hope that an angler or farmer would hear and take pity on me, but nothing more than a dry-throated rasp would come from my mouth. I suddenly wished that instead of thrashing the bottle over the German's head that I had simply taken a sip of the delicious liquid within.

The rain began to attack me horizontally, its cold and bitter manner seeping through the fibres of my clothes rapidly. To determine whether it was making its way through to my skin, I lifted my shirt gently and dabbed at my stomach.

It was getting through. I needed to get to my contact, otherwise, I could die from the elements now.

But, as I withdrew my palm from under my shirt, I realised that it wasn't just the elements that could kill me. It was the bleeding that had been dripping from somewhere for the entire time that I had been staggering through the field.

As I further inspected the source of the blood, desperately hoping that it was the wine that had somehow splashed over me, I realised that the German officer hadn't been such a bad shot after all.

He had missed on at least three attempts from

what I could make out. But at least two rounds had found their intended target; me.

My head suddenly began to loll from one side to the other as I berated myself for not noticing the wound sooner.

My hands flapped around urgently, as I stripped myself of my clothes to find my wounds.

From what I could see, which wasn't much on account of the volume of blood, was that I had one wound in my left hip, the other in the fleshy part of my side. It was a quick and easy explanation as to why I was finding it so difficult to traverse across the field.

It was only as I registered my wounds that the pain truly set in. I felt the colour drain from my face, my cheeks chilling, as did the tips of my fingers and toes. I felt like a ghost as I continued to move as much as I could, in order to prove to myself that I was still alive more than anything else.

But the pain was tremendous, and I fell down into the mud with a splash, simply allowing the pain to get the better of me. I let it fester for a moment or two, my body adjusting to the new kind of pain, before pulling myself along in the field, my left leg not working in perfect unison with my right any longer, managing only a few paces before I repeated the entire process again.

It was this process that I continued to repeat, over and over again, until I could smell that I was at the water's edge.

I closed my eyes, the pain subsiding ever so

slightly, as I grew more and more content with the eternal sound of the gushing water, just inches away from my head.

My eyes were heavy and cumbersome, and I struggled to lift them, but the noises around me were pricking my curiosity so much that I simply had to try and take in my surroundings.

I could not remember crossing the river that I had been lying next to, but I was aware that I was dry, in freshly laundered clothes and most importantly, warm. I wished that I could have added pain-free to that list, but that was most definitely not the case.

Lifting my eyelids, I could make out a face peering over me, how I imagined the first glimpses of heaven to be if I had ever made it there.

But as my eyes refocused, I realised that I couldn't have been in heaven. Not unless Philippe, the local policeman, had been taken from the mortal realms at some point that I had not been made aware of.

He smiled at me, a stupid toothy grin, that frustrated and angered me more than I could ever know. But I had no energy or inclination to want to move or do anything about his juvenile grinning face.

"Good morning," he said, as if it was the most natural thing in the world to be watching me waking up from my slumber.

"What happened?" I asked. "What's going on?" I

said, as I felt the bed that I was lying on jostling from side to side without my permission.

"We're moving you, Jean. Before the Germans get to close."

"You mean to say that they haven't caught me?"

He let out a hearty chuckle that bubbled away in the back of his throat.

"I should hope not!" he guffawed, resting a comforting hand on my shoulder. "As for what happened, well…this blood-soaked and fetid mess threw himself at my front door. Didn't even have the courtesy to knock…It was a good job you turned up when you did. Had it been five minutes later then I would have been on my way to church."

He chuckled again, as I closed my eyes with what I hoped was a smile, but my body was so numb I was not sure what I was able to do with my face.

"We're smuggling you into Switzerland. You should be safe from there. We aren't able to tell the others. It'll keep them safe as well as you."

My heart leapt at the thought that I was leaving France. It grew faster still at the thought that I was going to Switzerland. I could not recall saying anything in response to Philippe, but I heard his question loud and clear.

"Why's that? Who is Suzanne, my friend?"

I found it difficult to answer him, and so remained silent for a few minutes more, content to waft in and out of my sleep and spend my time trying to discern whether I was hallucinating, or if I was experiencing reality instead.

"Did you get there?" I asked, lifting my arm for the first time and patting Philippe somewhere that I hoped was his stomach.

"Did I get where, my friend?"

"C-church. Did you make it?"

My eyes were closed but I could tell that he was smiling a smile bigger than ever before.

"No! No of course I didn't. But I can tell you one thing, I've done more praying in the last few days than I ever have done in my life before."

I felt his body lean backwards, chuckling. My stretcher was still wobbling about from side to side, and I could now make out the vague chug of an engine not too far away. It was difficult to tell whether I was on some kind of a paddle steamer or in the back of a truck. I supposed it did not matter all that much. Just so long as the Germans didn't know either.

"Can you do me one more favour, Philippe?"

"Anything, my friend."

"Keep praying. Keep praying for my friend Mike."

The End…

For now.

ALSO BY THOMAS WOOD

Gliders over Normandy:

The Silent Invader

All Men are Casualties

As If They Were My Own

The Trench Raiders:

Slaughter Fields

Wavering Warrior

Invisible Frontline

Take Aim

Clouded Judgement

Long Forgotten

Alfie Lewis Thrillers:

The Evader

The Executioner

The Betrayed

Circuit Fortunae:

Don't Look Back

Playing with Fire

Close Quarters

www.ingramcontent.com/pod-product-compliance
Lightning Source LLC
Chambersburg PA
CBHW021620030826
48979CB00034B/486

* 9 7 8 1 9 1 6 4 1 3 8 7 0 *